I0616977

Adam Jacobs

the end as i know it

The Dot Wot

Published by The Dot Wot
ABN: 57566837638

ISBN 978-0-9875801-0-8

The Dot Wot

For my mother Margie, without which not, all my love.

For Simone, we speak with true abandon of love when laughter leaves us speechless.

For Rory Harris, sharer of talents. Thank you for your generosity and for giving this chronicle its coda.

Preface

I confess to writing this introduction with the desire to seed intuition and inform assumption.

This is a satire or, at least, satirical. It is not a story about God and it is not a story about Nature. It is a story about the end; some of the sophisticated endings a human must endure through the course of a lifetime. It may not be frivolous but it is not coercive, it does not mean to condition you with its interpretations, it means to interpret the human condition.

Literarily it must also be regarded as satirical, the profusion of alliteration, the plenitude of adverbs, the lexical density. However, it is not whimsy. The main protagonist, John Mathewson, is gifted with analysis and burdened with redundancy; such is the nature of his sympathy. Do not dismiss his attempts to be subtle as fancy; he would regard you for your idiosyncrasies and not for your commonalities. Do not dismiss his dissections as rarefied; he would ask that you regard him for his commonalities and not his idiosyncrasies. It is a catharsis and an attempt by him to turn his scientific means to a literary end. He aspires to give you all the shades of his meaning such as his means may provide.

A. Jacobs

Contents

confessional

Before I begin let me sacrifice a strength and confess a weakness: I am not equipped to recount this incident. There are others who are more masterful and gifted with craft, that are more literate and less hesitant, more given and less taken. They would make a better version of all the elementals and they would make a better version of me. However, I am trusted to speak personally of the protagonists and they would not expect that I should lend this inspiration to another. Therefore, respectfully, I will begin as I am inclined and hope that you will sacrifice my strengths as required. I indulge my weaknesses and hope you are also inclined to do so for, as you will discover, it comes to bear.

John Mathewson.

"War is foggy and it is true, the colder it is the foggier it becomes. The fog surrounding this war formed as the universe enjoyed its first dawn."

> J. Mathewson.
> *Warless - 1952.*

1

let there be light

Never had a day been so beautiful formed, a day like no other, like the very first or the very last. Its majesty should have transcended malevolence, an unsophisticated expectation but intrinsic. I recall feeling the sorcerous sting of that irony. It was a beguiling imposed by an edifying evolution that threatened to temper truth and pollute providence. Yes, unfortunately, a dark deception gives me greater reason to remember that beautiful day and not how singularly the sun shone or how sensibly the breeze blew. It is a day marred by complication, by didactic disturbance.

The 3rd of June 1834 was a glorious day, possibly, the sun shone and the breeze blew, maybe, lovely but no disturbance; unremarkable. The 12th of September 1954, however, was a beautiful day, definitely, and imperceptibly disturbed. It is remembered for what it failed to demonstrate and for not exclusively demonstrating beauty; such is the nature of my lament. However, I must not devalue the fortune gifted that day, the chance to reform the nucleus of my family after a remarkable disturbance. I am posing with my wife and our lovely children and the sun shone and the breeze blew.

How different the photograph might have been. Without the division of our nucleus the looks on our faces would not have expressed gratitude quite so honestly and the attitude of our bodies would not have been quite so forgiving, and the children? Would not have existed. What made that photographic opportunity exceptional was that it may never have been and not for the usual nucleus splitting reasons such as imminent world annihilation. No, the children, the man and his wife may never have come into a happy happenstance because the world demanded sperm, my sperm.

Or so I thought. This account must from the beginning begin, for if from the end? The necessary bestowing of plausibility on the implausible would render the plausible implausible. This type of story telling dilemma can be caused by only one kind of conundrum concocting crotchet known as, conspiracy. How else can a story marry together the turmoil of domesticity with imminent world annihilation?

But this subterfuge stands apart, it is qualified by an obscurity, a since retired characteristic of conspiracy known as the truth. Postwar Europe was an epoch defined by evincible guile, which paved the way for a very cold war. So how did a paranoia epidemic, progressive Nazism and my genetic material combine to bring about a photo opportunity that tells the story of civilisation's rebirth? It began in the surgery of my GP.

2

heaven and the earth

I had been ushered into the space, very familiar to me now. We greeted each other like equals, friends possibly but definitely with respect. It was doctor-patient but with a kind of shared understanding that I didn't always understand but I enjoyed the respect attending it.

•   •   •

I had managed to attract a considerable amount of respect. I was acknowledged within a small community of stimulated minds as a man ahead of his time. Not quite a science-fiction writer; a fortuneteller with a physics degree. Consequently a larger community of small-minded stimulants, who believed I was a science-fiction writer who had actually seen the future, worshiped me. They taught the world new fears. They introduced the world to conspiratorial conjecture, to chicanery theory. Ignorance may assume nothing but stupidity assumes everything.

So with their help I made a brave new world fearful of itself. The conspirators who sat on the side of science knew me as a theorist and the theorists that sat on the side of conspiracy wanted me to be a scientist. One group gave me respect reservedly and the other respected my reservations inconsistently. I wrote books essentially, that wallowed between fiction and non-fiction.

Non-fiction was my way of describing anything I wrote that failed to gain traction in the market place and fiction was my way of describing, reluctantly, a career.

I wrote about the future but I wasn't a writer, I forecasted. It was a dialogue that existed between my expectation and my readers' imagination that began, invariably, with the premise, *If everything continues as it is history will be inconsistently repeated.* Confounding specificity is it not? Astonishingly I helped motivate a new state of fear that germinated behind an iron curtain and seeded the paranoia of the brave, the free and the inequitable. I told the faithful what they wanted to hear and their faith demanded they hear more, *ad nauseam.*

For the most part, sitting by the fire watching the eddies and the seasons turn, shielded by the embrace of Oxford, the town and the University, I felt detached. I sat at my typewriter behind a wall of books and encouraged a war weary world to contemplate futures full of fictions. My little noise became a roar for no other reason except that a critical number of fatalists started listening. My voice rose above the commotion of greater turmoil because I was otherwise interested in the present and regarded fate with the base bemusement of the premature. This is how revolutions and holocausts incubate. Exactly why they listened was beyond my ability to fully understand, except that mixing science with fiction has the effect of turning an untrustworthy world upside down, changing disconcertion into science and befuddlement into faith.

But this story is not concerned directly with my pseudo-scientific manuscripts, though it comes to bear. This story is mostly concerned with the recording of other data, my genetic data.

•   •   •

Dr. Richardson made all the usual assessments,

"You are a picture of health, you and I both know the issue is not yours," he stated predictably.

"I know," I responded; it was habitual.

Every month I subjected myself to the assessment and every time the results told me what I already knew, our inability to conceive a child was a failing I was unable to burden. However, the agreement I made with my wife Carmen required me to provide samples every month for analysis. I was not nagged nor niggled. It was assumed with immense confidence that I would do what was necessary. Every month Dr. Richardson subjected me to a process of elimination and every month the possibility that I might be defective was categorically eliminated.

My fertile status was of some comfort to Carmen. It had the potential however, to open a divide between us too great to bridge. It is possible to over water with optimism the seedling of hope.

Optimism becomes less affiliated with reality the more it is relied upon to bolster belief in things we cannot control. I stood by and watched as desperation tempted her towards a mirage. With a casting of sympathy and a reeling of instinct I could have pulled her free of her anguish. It would have been a consolation for a childless future she might have pretended to accept. However, I did not want her to sense acrimony or have to, 'till death us do part, tolerate me sycophantically pruning her guilt from my resentment.

I could never have told her the true nature of my sentiment. To be a father would be fulfilling. To not be one did not mean, however, I would remain incomplete. Completeness was an idea, a modus vivendi I had adopted. It described ageing in a way that was not informed by continuances such as children. It was simply an acknowledgment that to go on as I was, at that moment, was a complete and unaffected experience. It allowed for an intimate appreciation of time. Time will tolerate the imposition as self seeks completion so long as the completion is definitive otherwise time will plague the individual with hubris. Subsequently, death must be unfettered by lineage and be preoccupied with the métier of God.

I was of course fooling myself. I was masking the realities of regret with the propaganda of selfishness. It is however, not far removed from the state of being I submerge into when I write. I become the embodiment of time, swaying to its measures. Writing is a meditation, not always easy to maintain but it will consume self, often confusing its ambitions.

I acknowledged that self was the social enabler that necessitated procreation and was stimulated by the regard of its needs. But the subsequent dissonance was intolerable and I was caused to resolve - the world does not necessitate more from me than I am inclined to give presently, and presently, Carmen is replenished by the knowledge that I am viable.

3

then there was man

For more than a year I had been making the pilgrimage to the Doctor. I was told what I already knew and my relationship with him was on autopilot. But on this occasion he was regarding me differently, with an eye that seemed better suited to a dog show or to judge a bull at the county auction. He was assessing the proportions, the distributions and the densities. I suspected he suspected I did not notice. I waited and said nothing for I predicted it would come to something promptly.

My suspicions were confirmed. Towards the end of the consultation he took up a file and removed a document, he turned the pages and hesitated. He appeared to know what needed to be said but not how he needed to be saying it. *I look back at that fateful moment and I see irony. I see the scientist attempt to talk science-fiction with the fictional scientist.*

He began,

"I have been asked, when I say *I*, I mean many Doctors...most, I suspect. We have been...required to pay particular attention to certain," he read from the document, "...physical specimens who present as genetically..."

He hesitated again, reconsidering his decision to quote directly from the form. *Genetic superiority* was not quite a stigmatised term but it made many post-war eyebrows twitch. It was very much associated with a war not forgotten, with Nazism, with Hitler, with grotesque biological grandstanding that used science as propaganda to tell us lies and truths we were not yet prepared to hear. The theories were flawed, the practices brutal and the objectives unachievable. What did happen however, was an awakening. The world learnt that not all men were created equal, not unless they were created to be equal. Men could play God but first they needed demigod specimens to run through their maze of blood work and vivisections before Nature's secrets could be counterfeited.

I almost didn't need to be told anymore and Dr Richardson knew it,

"I feel like I don't need to tell you anymore," he obliged.

I also didn't need to be told,

"The wars of the future John will be fought under the microscope."

It was not said so I might enhance my collection of things I didn't need to be told, he said it in an attempted to cure his awkwardness. With a tonal shift and a peppering of projection the words suddenly belonged to the confident professional that I knew him to be, that's not to suggest it wasn't rehearsed.

Under the microscope? It is the only efficient means for breeding an army. But the war had already begun. It was fought between bed sheets by lovers and the outcome was evolution. Or procreation or population growth eventuating in a crossbred revolution, a coitus contaminated cultural insurrection. As the difference between the races becomes less discernible so will the purposes of war. It is true that prejudice has a very long shelf life but in a staring competition genetics wins. Prejudice will become a ghost rambling impotently about in the basement of our instincts.

War, like all of technology's exclamations, has only one objective, to become microscopic. This dumb thumping around we demonstrate with bombs and guns will give way to a far more sophisticated means of confrontation, an invisible means. Biological superiority will determine an outcome so inconsequential that philosophers will be asked to determine the result and submit a monthly report. The greatest of all philosophical statements is war. It is sophistic and subsequently difficult to conceive an end to it. How can an end be defined within a frame of reference that exists exclusively to reference the frame? War is evolution learning patience as it attempts to hurry things along. It turns like the seasons and is perpetual. It can't be arrested but it may be muted. Without war humanity's -*ity* becomes redundant, purpose would no longer necessitate society and continuance would be voided.

War will evolve into a tokenistic endeavour

executed by intellectuals who will rely upon the physical laws of the universe to engineer outcomes. The winner will receive temporary validation and the loser will become a stakeholder in a refocused campaign. There will be more than two world wars; there'll be thousands, new ones every week that constantly realign allegiances.

●　　●　　●

So what window onto a microscopic war was Dr Richardson asking me to peer through? An answer to that question was instantly apparent, one that illuminated the fabric of my design.

"We must be prepared," he continued, his awkwardness had returned.

I saw my moment; a display of ignorance might milk out of him some particulars,

"Why me?"

"You are strong in body and mind," he countered enthusiastically relieved to have been given permission to be out-with-it,

"You are fertile and the right age. I simply would like to put your details forward for consideration. They may accept you or they may not. If they do you will be asked to attend The Institute where they will conduct some tests, nothing too invasive."

He said all this in such a rush and was so clearly relieved to have said it that once it had been said I was led to ponder - what has he not said?

But my initial analysis was reactionary and from the confusion of his babble the words *The Institute* leapt into my awareness. He would have avoided naming the place I suspect; nervous energy had usurped his discretion. But those words had been spoken and I felt they put me more clearly in the picture and so much the better. I certainly didn't need to be told that The Institute consisted of a team of highly scientific manipulators tasked with the highly scientific manipulating mission to answer the highly scientific manipulated question, can humans be engineered? I also didn't need to be told that I would be expected to help provide an answer.

From that fateful moment onwards it could not be said that I was not to blame for my engagement in that highly scientific manipulation. It was as if I had been invited into a parable I had worried from my very own pen. How could I say no? It was as if someone who had read my books, and had chosen to entertain the science and discredit the fiction, had devised this initiative. There must be others, other participants would be required but this was not a question for Dr. Richardson.

With little hesitation I gave him my approval. His eyebrows twitched with mild surprise and, with a vigour I had not seen before, he sprang to his feet, began flicking through the manual and ticking boxes. He said the assessment was cursory but, after measuring every part of my body and asking an array of perplexing questions, an hour and fifteen minutes had passed. He informed me that upon our next meeting he would surely have a response. I went home and had a very familiar lie to tell and a truth to keep secret.

14

4

the rib

She stood at the sink. Her preoccupation with the dishes was maddening. In so many ways she was Nature's child, sympathetic and intuitional. But if a dish was dirty then it required exactly three minutes of her obsessive devotion. The house was tidy, as always, and her square cut linen dress, a fashion void, moved hypnotically with the washing motion. She had trouble making sense of a world that had moved away from Nature. It seemed a strange kind of retraction that, after the expansion of war, the world should be bent on bending backwards to beatify technology.

Tokens of her love of Nature were scattered throughout the house, a horde of amateur archeological possessions. Fertility symbols mostly, from all corners of the earth. Fertility was the elephant in the room, but exposed, we didn't regard him directly. It was not so much that she had trouble accepting that our inability to conceive was a failure she alone should own. It was more that she could not comprehend why Nature should abandon one of its ardent devotees. She knew Mother-earth as well as one of Nature's fixtures might be inclined. Carmen was the bird and the stone, air and water. She was fire and wind, sand and the trees.

But she was obsessed. Compulsion had plagued her for many years. It forced her to keep an ordered eye on everything including her collection of invocatory tokens; the entrance hall resembled a museum. The compulsions forced her to apply order where Nature needed none and to ignore chaos where Nature needled neatness. The house was a picture of uniformity but her hair was a bird's nest, clean but falling about in loose curls, constantly catching her lips and eyelashes, its wiry bun slipping to one side and full of miniature coils of conflict. Her factory-woman style attire was in keeping with her hair and made working in the garden or collecting the firewood less obstructed, it strategically discouraged socialisation.

I stood in the doorway, made observations and expected detection. I am not sure if it was motivated by my morning's peculiarity but as I stood and admired her idiosyncrasies I evolved a new understanding. Freedom was in her habitude and was allowed to tease her peripheries; it represented an earth energy, the mothering wilds. The compulsions and neatness represented a need to contain that energy, which once released may take her too far from self and its addiction to me. She had attached an externalisation of that freedom to the notion of giving birth. I concluded that her love of the natural world intensified the guilt caused by her innate reluctance to yet burden bairn. The agony of the irony saddened me as I considered how I might be contributing to her turmoil; I almost failed to reciprocate her acknowledgment.

I couldn't entirely understand her self-imprisonment but some inclination told me it was the core of our problems. I had returned from my regular pilgrimage to the doctor with the same story to tell of bittersweet confirmations. We had learnt not to go subtly pointing the finger. We had had numerous, emotionally sophisticated conversations, politely establishing that our problem with conceiving a child begins and ends with her. So we waited, as many couples had done before us, and hoped that something as banal as the passing of time might be the miracle we were seeking.

I hesitated before I told her about the more unusual part of my morning's medical meandering. Genetic experimentation and fertility issues are somewhat too analogous for the purposes of small talk. I had this notion that, fuelled by paranoia, she may suspect, with Dr. Richardson's assistance, I had determined to let science make certain use of my genetic material, let science do what she appeared unable to achieve. I chose my words carefully,

"I was a lab-rat today dear."

"Should I be surprised?" She wasn't.

"Definitely," I continued. "Dr Richardson has some use for my measurements. He noted all my dimensions and made ticks in boxes and many moans of approval."

"Surely not?" She provided rhetorically.

"...or disapproval, I couldn't be entirely sure," I concluded.

"It's not always easy to know the difference, moans are notoriously ambiguous," she said as she gave me a squeeze full of all the yearning the remnants of her youth could afford.

Youth was charging us more, especially for displays of yearning, and for the first time in my life I was beginning to see myself as what I would become and not as I once might have been. I assumed that time played a similar beat across the membrane of her awareness. We stood holding each other as the afternoon sun slowly began to close its eye. For one peculiar moment I felt that we were dancing to the same lamenting chime, a tick tock that reverberated with the distant hum of adolescence.

She sprang away from me, as was her occasional form, and with the aid of imitation pleaded once more that we should have a dog. It pleased me that it pleased her and, if it were not for bureaucratic procrastination, I am certain we would have already been a family of three.

The house belonged to the University and requests for pets had to be made formally, be considered at meetings, be drafted into leases and be made a very big something of so redundancy might masquerade merit. I had never encountered such an over governed arrangement and the end result shall be an animal we might call our own. With all the bother it would cost us it might have felt somewhat as if we were actually giving birth to the critter ourselves.

It will be called Rama, a name borrowed from a Malay-Indian connection Carmen's family once enjoyed. She suggested it might be a German Short-haired Pointer, homage to the gun dogs from her childhood. I favoured Greyhounds but they are lazy. I did not pretend to have any power to influence the decision. The choice of dog breed and the decision when we should breed were apparently two consequences that I was not able to inform directly.

5

the house of god

Dr. Richardson was prophetic. The response from The Institute was resounding. I would be a guaranteed inclusion into their program. It is a strange sensation to have one's hidden qualities so convincingly applauded. My genetic potential was essential to the program's operation. Dr. Richardson saw no reason to not read directly from the letter being sure to emphasise the importance they placed on his initiative. He was clearly proud and I got the impression that it afforded him a degree of kudos. I am not sure, now that I make this recollection if he, like me, gave into a quizzical hesitation upon hearing the word *potential*. It suggested that some essence of me might be extracted and utilised for quests beyond my reckoning. Regardless, at that moment, we celebrated.

We smiled at each other with a kind of bemusement and the raising of astonished eyebrows, which equated to a very polite slap on the back. It then struck me how very English we were. We are a race of colonisers and much colonising had been achieved with the waving of the Union Jack. Achieved in a manner disproportionately polite considering the devastation our progress initiated. I was caused to cogitate - this endeavour may place me on the front line of a new infiltration.

• • •

Only one frontier remains to be claimed, space, or the heavens, a more suitable term. Not that I wish to suggest that I am referring to God, except that I am referring to God. The omnipresent territory that God claims as his will be colonised. With the magical swirl of a test tube the entire domain of existence can be formulated. Under microscopes the entire story of God's greatest creation is exposed, a creation that, blessed with awareness, brought all things into the mystery of consciousness. This life force, the same force that God gave form to on the sixth day, in his own likeness, now hopes to emulate the Father. He hopes to conjure, in his own likeness, counterfeits.

It is a particular interest of mine to bring together space and God. Ultimately, we will evolve into space, into *a* space. It is our destiny to fill a universe entirely and it is inevitable. I refer to a conceptual expanse that says more about our ability to evolve an awareness of self than it does about our ability to literally move heaven and earth. This space is boundless and it is trapped within. Meditations will reveal the limitlessness of this internal territory and it invites expeditions that we are all capable of launching. The ability of the mind to be without occupation, to be momentarily consumed with nothing, to be forced into vacuity, this is the summit of self-awareness and the true meaning of space.

God knows us as space-invaders, as navigators through the void. The investigation begins in our awareness and will ultimately consume our imagination. This *inner-verse* is the sketchpad upon which the brutish animal we are scribbles the rude shape of the social Being that we must become to survive. It is also the birthplace of hypotheses revealing, in the form of a question, that which we know not of but must be reconciled to. Curiosity compels us. It is the tool God has given to remind us that self-awareness is his way of enabling our sense of science.

Can I imagine, in many decisive years to come, that men and women may sit in spacecrafts and look out at a distant Earth and presume that God might have adopted a similar position as he rendered his grand design? Can I suppose it is not hubris to suppose such things? So science is God leading us to water and hoping that we will analyse it.

● ● ●

The Institute was the house of God in which I would sacrifice my weaknesses and confess my strengths and all for science, all for the purposes of engineering a perfect example of imperfection.

6

revelation

The nondescript envelope contrasted proportionally with the significance of its contents. To leave the surgery with it stabbed securely under my arm gave me a sense of belonging. I now belonged to a genuine initiative; my fictionalising had been rendering travesties. I would not have admitted that the fortuneteller aspect of my work demonstrated a desire I had to stake a claim in a real scientific frontier, except that almost everything I did existed to demonstrate a desire I had to stake a claim in a real scientific frontier. It is something quite different to be directly informing the future as opposed to sharing the details of a dream with the informers of the future.

●　　●　　●

They quip, as they are often inclined to, those who can *do*, and those who can't *teach*. It is a concept I have never found the means to agree with. I am not regarded as a teacher, though my sense of self tells me that I am very much a teacher, entirely a teacher. More to the point my observation of teachers causes me to adjust that quip, those who can *teach*, and let those who *do* try. It has been my experience that we are all teachers, maintaining our ability to *do* involves demonstrating our ability to *teach*.

●   ●   ●

I had grown tired however, of being the one who knows everything about things most of us will not live long enough to appreciate. The Institute was offering me the chance to fill the here and now with the future, my future. It was the scientific equivalent of imagining my cake and eating it too.

But before I conceptualised my cake I would have to inform Carmen. I had been reticent, even misleading and now it was time to explain. My absence would be undeniable and my distraction alienating. I would have to present an argument, tell some truths and some lies and suggest that now might be a good time for her to adopt a hobby. Not that she relied on me to distract her from the banal but I was a prominent fixture in her daily operations.

She was tormented by fastidious distractions and did not welcome change. I feared that she would become more introverted. *Later I would learn something about enabling. For years I had been contributing to her disability and I had only but my good intentions to blame.*

I entered the house in the usual manner and she greeted me accordingly. The Elephant in the room now took the form of an oversized envelop under my arm. It shifted self-consciously and fell to the floor. She picked it up and handed it to me. However, her grip did not immediately relax. The anonymous envelope led her into a moment's distraction, which broke only when I gave a small tug and she surrendered it. She looked a question at me but said nothing, smiled then turned away. She may have recognised the stationary, Dr. Richardson's stock and may have wondered if I had made an unscheduled visit. She did however, assume ignorance which led me into a hesitation - who was lying to whom?

Delicate deceptions had become very much apart of our relationship's sustenance. White lies had been adopted to mitigate the pain of our childless reality. Contrition, betrayed by apology, was tolerated because we loved each other. Love had been the veneer behind which we could hide and not fear the truth. No degree of analysis however, could pacify our uneasiness in any way like the arrival of a child might.

But something was different, there was the envelope, it was suspicious. It was a lie that she had chosen not to challenge and it was the permission we needed to begin a new deception. She returned to the kitchen. I made my way into the dinning area and began my explanation by recycling some Shakespeare,

"Nothing so becomes a man..."

"But when he hears the blast of war," she augmented the quote and took her seat as I retorted,

"True, more true than most men would likely admit."

"Admit to but still relish. It's supposed to be warm, the salad with Pumpkin, it's Moroccan."

The spices exploded in my mouth. She didn't

want to change the subject but she knows I am a culinary voyeur.

She enjoys my indirect approach, especially if she suspects I might broach a discomforting subject. It's consensual; I'm not inclined to come directly to the point. I might begin by stirring-in some literary sugar; it adds favour to the flavour of my indirection. She enjoys the lettered fumbling that I occasionally adopt. It gives her the opportunity to remind me that she is the literary master and I'm nothing more than a master literalist.

My dumb playing-around with archaic sayings may have been unpolished but it placed me in an intellectually subordinate position; I made good use of the empathy it garnered.

She threw me a suspicious glance, amorous and peppered with an effortless sensuality. It's a look that evolves into tenderness once a woman becomes a mother and I am compelled, momentarily, to contemplate destiny. I knew the time had come to spill my beans,

"I'll be absent entirely...for the duration."

I spilt the words, disrespecting the tabletop delicacies but she found the forthrightness palatable,

"A duration? That long? I can't say I'm surprised."

"Why?" I asked genuinely.

"It's that time again," she sighed.

"Yes," I sympathised.

I didn't know entirely what she meant but I was entirely certain that she meant it.

"Three weeks, not long," I concluded.

She returned to her plate distracted, smiling? It might have been a simper. It was a resignation acknowledging that having her suspicions confirmed was not an adequate price to pay for the temporary loneliness I had assigned her to. She gave into the sadness but not purely because our relationship must endure new restrictions. No, she knew that change was immanent. She would have to accept that this new loneliness was a catalyst. Issues relating to want and need must be addressed, it would be a painful process.

I was certain that resolution, for so long spoiled by procrastination, at that moment came to bear. Her lament was not so much to do with my abandonment. But she maintained her composure, as she had become accustomed to do. With another sigh and a stir of her fork I very much got the impression that she had resolved to evolve, to somehow give up the compulsions and be free. In that one unspoken moment fate figured. It suggested I would not be returning to the Carmen with which I shared that final refection.

It felt as if anything worth us saying would best be insinuated. No other means meted this more mercilessly than our unspoken moments. We were not disabled by denial. We had had all the conversations, we had said all the words, we had trampled all over the territory of the explicit and there was nothing left to be left unsaid. So we had to go beyond, into new regions. We lived in a fog, daring each other to stretch the safety line of cohabitation. We would intentionally lose sight of each other, and then reconnect with a tongue-in-cheek hoot or mocking animal call. It was a perilous way to operate. It encouraged an incremental alienation, a painless parting. We had adopted sympathetic distances relative to each other's habits as we began to find a means to a childless end. Our ageing selves had to find an enduring modus operandi and we chose euphemism and wit. But now I would be absent and the metaphysical distance between us would become materially physical. But we both felt it more like a cosmic thing, but not mystically cosmic, it was theoretical. We were future dwellers finding a way to coexist without the notions of *us* and *we* to force procreation.

● ● ●

Everything expands. The stars are racing away from each other. War had adopted distance choosing to make moves from behind curtains that shaded revolutions and borders that fenced in freedom. The future will be a place where friendship is determined by a tick in a box and technology will be a buffer. One that allows for the worst of human behaviour to ejaculate into virtual nothingness, giving birth to cookie cutter individuals obsessed with individualism...

...If nothing else I expected to enjoy a respite from the bleak predictions my research had recently encouraged me to entertain.

● ● ●

Carmen knew opportunity was rapping on the

ramparts and we would have to give up the complacency we called love. We hoped that a different kind of love would come back in its place. Nothing worth attaining is gained without risk and we had chosen, in one unspoken moment, to risk it all.

7

before time

The instructions were simple, arrive at Kings Cross Station and proceed to Omicron for departure at 8.55am. I left Oxford, made the necessary change and arrived at Kings Cross with time enough to cure my amnesia. It had been almost eighteen months since I had been to London and more than three years since I had been to Kings Cross Station. But like most public spaces the flow of it informs your instincts like a compass. The architects and their anthropology appear to know you better than you know yourself and, consequently, I became quickly reoriented.

What I did not have time for was Omicron. Not a platform in a station anywhere in the world is surely indicated by the Greek letter of O and naught else. It was a code, a hidden indicator leading the way down the rabbit hole. It was a needle in the hay, in agitated silage.

But why? Attempting to unravel this codified instruction, having no specific notion of what The Institute was hypothesising, led me to question my aptitude in more than one way. I was led to seek this Omicron based on an assumption of what I believed The Institute intended for me. If Omicron led me to expose the hatter's hatch should I go ignorantly across its threshold, be distracted by pride and posture victoriously? Or should I observe that distracting me with my own conceit was their first objective? If so it is not unreasonable to assume the more hesitant this symbol hunt should force me to be might proportionally indicate the severity of their intended invasiveness. I had been warned. There was only one cure for the quandary my intellectual fidgeting had invented. The ardent science-fictionalist in me must step forward and declare, *go boldly for nothing shall come of nothing*.

However, I had no idea how the Greek letter *O* might be represented in a colossal train station in a way that would guide me towards my departure in a timely manner. I crossed the concourse and conjectured - they chose to use Omicron? But why not Omega or Sigma, both are far more discernible? Why should our inclusion in their scheme be predicated on such rude measures? So we may be the animal first, target driven and impulse primed? Then be the analyst and take apart the animal we are?...Yes.

I had never been sent on such a mission before and, consequently, I never before noticed how many *O*'s a train station is inclined to accommodate. They were simply everywhere and one of them, supposedly, had reason to be sensible to my intelligence but for no reason I could sensibly

31

fathom. Shortly after beginning my search I ceased looking for the obvious and began to seek the obscure, and then I abandoned the obscure and looked again at the obvious but in a more obscure manner, and that gave way to an observation of the act of observing and a subsequent procrastination concerning the observation of procrastination. It seemed hopeless and I was about to chastise myself for lax preparation or some latent failing when a grubby little circle appeared within the shadowy recess of an abandonment.

The featureless door that it sat above cracked open and another shaft of light threw itself upon the obscured *O*. It may have once been apart of a word or a number but now it was nothing more than passé graffiti. I had found it and also discovered that it lead the way for many others besides me. I observed two then three people, officious types, pass through the door. I surveyed the throng of passersby and suddenly felt vulnerable. Objectively there was nothing amiss with the exiting of these commuters from the concourse, nothing suspicious essentially. It was not the typical means for accessing a platform but there were always exceptions, maintenance works to avoid and the like. So why did I feel inhibited? Unworthiness? I clipped the notion hard but the insinuation teased some innate inadequacy; with a deep breath and a long blink I was restored.

The station crowd consisted of people with somewhere to go and an eager need to get there. I knew where I was going but my need was not yet informed. I expected there would be others waiting, as I was, for the impetus. I could file in behind sympathetically, once they had vanquished vacillation; it was cowardly. However, the chaos of moving bodies appeared to obscure other temporisers and so self-consciousness impeded. Then a group of arrivals cleared and I saw her. She was one of them, one of us, she must have been? She stood staring at the door. We were two motionless entities in a space filled with organised chaos. She turned and our eyes met.

In one movement and with clear intent she turned and looked at me squarely. I was somewhat spooked to have been sighted so precisely and my vanity postured - am I recognised? Another group passed between us and then she was gone. I turned and saw someone enter the opening. I moved towards the closing door with unrehearsed composure which gave way to a pang of superstition - if I didn't make it to the door before it closed again then it may not open for me. I reached for the lever and with a nervous jerk misplaced my hand. I cleared the handle and as my knuckle rushed past I nudged it affecting the door's sound closure. I was flummoxed by my farcical fumble and wasn't sure what to do next; a hand came in next to me. It belonged to the woman on the concourse. She looked at me and said nothing. Her unaffected countenance belied an anthropological tolerance of human animals. She was earnest but unperturbed. It was Miriam, our first encounter. She led me across the threshold and into her destiny. The door swung open and instantly I was blinded.

The brilliant light within needed accommodating and, like the others I had seen enter, I paused for a moment before bridging the breach. The imposition of the luminosity forced me to act out some hesitation. I paused, squinted and shuffled, dazed and revealed. Most disconcerting until I realised that the source of the light was nothing more than a workman's lamp. I tipped my hat and masked the intensity revealing the truth behind the cheap theatrics. The glare led the way down a dirty flight of stairs effectively but did nothing to mask the smell. The odour was horrid, dank, mouldy and something else, maybe death. The tunnel must have been recently pumped free of stagnate buildup; storm water and who knows what else.

It was a disused line. There were many of them and, in accordance with their subterranean aspect, they were often filled with waste. This one had very recently been recommissioned for no other reason, or so it seemed, than to ferry my kind and me to the innovative noviciate we would call home for the next two weeks.

8

creation

We start behind the scenes. The Institute was essentially a back-of-house operation and we were ushered in through the service entrance. We were not just behind the scenes we were compelled to wheel them about, push upon the rails and the flat and make the canvas move across the stage. Before we could admit ourselves into the maze we were required to build the maze. By *we* I mean a multitude. Apparently Great Britain was teaming with genetic marvels, I had become a face in a very exclusive crowd. We all had the same question teasing our frontal lobes - has the competition begun? The fittest must survive and so too, apparently, must the fittest of the fittest.

We were required to build the maze ourselves and by that I mean, we were required to build the maze ourselves. Yes, inside an anonymous industrial space stood a considerable collection of able bodied, bright minded minions. The entire space had been emptied of its industrial gizzards and painted white. The massive doors were boarded with a splash of firetruck red. There was a portable stage, a microphone on a stand and a desk with a typewriter. We stood empty-handed and empty-headed waiting for the colossal space to reveal a secret or encourage some response.

From the far end of the building a door clicked open and three men appeared followed by a young, high heel-clicking woman. She carried a small stack of folders and wore an army uniform. The others paraded the finest in shapeless lab coats except for the first; he wore black. It was a suit, tailored but featureless. He also wore an eyepatch and I supposed patriotic misadventure. The two white mice and the dame took their place on the stage. The woman sat at the typewriter and clicked a fresh page into the mechanism. The man in black ascended with controlled anticipation, walked deliberately to the microphone and never once took his eye from us. He paused and the girl clicked and I assumed, as I am sure we all did, that the date and time had been noted.

"Welcome."

We were all visibly surprised to hear that he was not British. When I say we were all visibly surprised it was a typically invisible English visibly surprised that we shared in a typical invisibly English visible manner. That is, we almost turned to look at each other, almost.

The Americans were our allies but we were not *in-bed*. Bedfellows made strange comrades, mainly because Hitler was no longer able to move the pillow talk away from ego-driven self-interest. There was a new *them and us*. This collaboration was unexpected and so too was this American's quiet but insidious style of communication.

"Welcome," he continued, "The Institute is fortunate to have secured your inclusion. Your contribution shall, without exaggeration, help redefine the human condition. This space will become a testing ground where the latest in behavioural, biochemical and genetic scientific understanding will be extended towards achieving the ultimate advancement our species has known. I am Alistair Dulaney, United States Army Intelligence and this is your facility."

With a kind of misplaced ceremony the massive doors on one side of the building yawned open and trucks, crates and machines began pouring in. The commotion ceased with rehearsed abruptness.

One of the lab coats standing behind Dulaney stepped forward, snatched up the folders and began disseminating them randomly to my disorientated comrades. Dulaney explained,

"Most of you are the operators of this experiment, a few of you are the subjects and your first task is to determine, which is your destiny. The information contained in these files will allow for the creation of a facility tasked with a very specific responsibility. The equipment, this space, this time is what your government and mine require to make key determinations that will inform an uncertain future. May God be with you."

The last statement was thrown out across the commotion of the abstracted and was carefully recorded by the typist, as had every one of his words. The impatient multitude had begun their devotion and was otherwise concerned as to the whereabouts of God.

I watched Dulaney and the others exit unceremoniously. I had listened to his words and the meaning behind them and the hidden meanings behind those meanings and I felt a fatalistic twinge. It's the same twinge I feel before I begin a new unit of work or research. I felt a new America was on display before us. In the habitude of this war veteran I saw something damaged but shrewd, intelligent but not necessarily wise, persuasive and prone to literalism. On him I projected a vision of the U.S.A as an uncompromising power, gifted with the ability to say what is necessary and package it with a potent but redundant dogma.

The typist followed the American obediently as she stole glances across the room; she caught my eye. We shared a look, she turned away smartly and I was left feeling like there was something we were not being told. Someone pushed past me and, as I was shunted back into the moment, I realised that there were many things we had not been told. Precisely, we had not been told anything. We had been given a folder; a typed tendering and we were expected to motivate the advancement of the species by joining dots.

I began to survey the commotion more carefully. All manner of human inclinations were on display. The folders were being handed one to the other, pages being pulled this way and that. Others were unpacking trucks and scratching their heads. Three ascended the stage to make use of the desk and typewriter. Hierarchies were being established, implied understandings were becoming specialties, thinkers were being separated from the doers and the observers, like me, were becoming a very small minority.

Then a very odd moment emerged, very odd indeed. The documents had been circulated, an understanding had been adopted and the ignorant had been left to flounder. With the effect of some indiscernible wave the commotion of organisation subsided, a synchronised awakening forced everyone into an eerie stasis.

There were six left standing in the centre of the space and everyone was staring at us. The typewriter was rendered motionless, so were the spanners and the callipers, the pencils and the test tubes. One of the three on the stage descended and took a lab coat from a rack; he slipped it over his shoulders as he walked towards a small group of technicians. He whispered something to the one who held the clipboard. She responded obsequiously and, with a series of gestures and inaudible commands, her team set to sorting a pile of clothes and moving the furniture. Six members of her team stepped forward to where my five fated friends and I had chosen to congregate.

One by one we were taken by the arm and escorted to a furnished area. Screens were brought in around us, hospital beds were wheeled into place and within minutes our new home, and its medically

39

informed decor, had been clearly established. With the pull of a curtain I was isolated. The pyjamas sitting on the end of the bed told me what my next task should be. I began to undress and fell into a meditation. The pieces of a contradiction began to align and took the form of something resembling irony. We were charged with a task that pointed, possibly, to the salvation of the human race but first we had to assign importance to a redundant Greek symbol in a train station, endure cheap theatrics, run a sewer stained gauntlet, be told by an American what to do, erect the walls, demystify the science and objectify our compatriots. That the salvation of the human race should be made up of less inglorious ingredients is desirable but was, apparently, incongruent.

9

mysterious ways

Conviction of purpose had been forced upon me, a concoction of very potent temptations had been created with the express purpose of engineering my addiction. The Institute was everything that the scientist in me had hypothesised and everything the dreamer in me had hallucinated. It consumed me with a very male kind of yearning that is fantasy driven and outcome motivated. To answer the question, what compels men to obsess? One must first ask rhetorically, is a problem ever truly solved? Men are intrinsically sophistic. They demonstrate the ability possessed by humans to be demonstrative. Subsequently what they are not is sophisticated. Males will pause to admire and admire the pause; they are both dogs chasing tails and tails teasing dogs.

Something primal in males makes us want to solve problems and often with little regard for the true value of the consequences. Fate had given me what I had asked for and all it asked in return was that I risk everything I love.

Carmen's purpose would necessitate a different kind of motivation. She had a modus and conviction but their alignment would require an extraordinary act of fate. Witchcraft is a science. Any witch worth her coven will tell you that alchemy, divination, prophecy and potions are first scientific enterprises. Witchcraft and science are beautifully aligned because they both acknowledge the impermanence of everything with the exception of energy. With the startling intervention of a bewitched science Carmen would become enlightened regarding the permanent nature of energy and its ability to flow.

● ● ●

This begins the story within my story. The intimate details of which I enjoy intimate access to. Accordingly please accept the sometimes-omniscient nature of the narration. Poetry has meaning, meaning has truth, truth is freedom and freedom is poetry and so fiction, is liberated fact.

● ● ●

While I made the world prepared for an uncertain but highly manipulated future Carmen was receiving an insider's tour of Nature and her forces. I would be relocated to London for three weeks; this gave Carmen time and space. She had no notion of what to do with either of those gifts but she knew they must be exploited extensively.

I caught the train on Monday at 5:50am and Carmen endured the remainder of the day acclimatising to the solitude. That evening she made her regular pilgrimage to the town library. She volunteered after hours to shelve books. It was an opportunity for her to be in the company of socialisers without enduring the expectation to participate. She would linger in the dusty recesses of non-fiction and allow herself to be distracted by botanical texts, specifically, anything relating to the ingestion of plant life. She had become fascinated by the power of plants to heal, affect, maim and kill.

It comes to bear. Her barrenness was not within the realms of mainstream science to cure and so she had become obsessively interested in the alternatives. In the process she had discovered a happy distraction that lead her away from longing and into malevolent entertainments - how could an unobtrusive spec of a weed be processed to produce such a noxious result that it might kill a grown person? Many of these plants are not legally allowed to bloom in the repose of civilised beds. That does not mean they will not germinate in the hedgerows of cultivated madness.

She was kneeling on the carpet; in a pose not unlike the kind she adopted in the garden or at church, and was considering a strange weed known for its need to be avoided. In the distance simmered the soft murmur of conversation putting her sense of loneliness into hibernation. However, the security of her isolation was rudely shown for an illusion when Buki appeared,

"You don't want to be using the likes of that for anything I might consume."

She was larger than Carmen, physically and in every other way, and she spoke with a strong

43

Jamaican accent.

"Pardon?"

Carmen closed the book with the nervous automation indicative of a child with one hand discovered in the cookie jar. Buki, barely concealing her amusement declared,

"My girl, I'm not asking you nothing but to make better choices if ever you suppose to sup with me. That herb there, that you were just now considering, it'll give you strange thoughts and bad dreams. But you keep reading, I'm not here to stop you, except to ask for a moments assistance."

Buki began to consider Carmen more carefully. It was not impertinence it was inclination. Buki had been in the company of the needy long enough to recognise, almost instantly, those who required her specialised assistance.

She had been in Oxford for less than a week. Her sister had made her a home and at once Buki felt that this town was needy. Buki knew how to cook and to conjure, two very scientific endeavours, and longed to make a contribution. She would begin by conducting classes teaching traditional Jamaican recipes accommodating very modern French techniques. That evening she had pinned a poster onto the library notice board, her first cooking class would commence tomorrow night and all were welcome. She then had the need to peruse the non-fiction. Her sister had the space for vegetables and herbs but not the inclination to cultivate them. Buki saw it as her first duty to put the garden right. Soon enough she would be cooking for one of the residential halls and so, whilst she had the time and inclination, she would do the garden a favour.

The library was closed and the librarians regarded her with unmitigated discomfort but she was admitted. Buki's personable way made asking permission for almost anything purely a courtesy. She was unable to be refused, or so it seemed. She would insist that Carmen attend her cooking class,

"Girl, I seek a book on planting, anything that will help me make sense of this English weather. I'll be putting in herbs and vegetables. The ground has good light but not a finger of love has been put to it; it's just grass all over, very green English grass. No good for eating unless you a cow or a goat and I'm not planning on being either."

Buki made this request and some additional observations whilst Carmen began selecting texts for her consideration.

Carmen rose slowly, unable to resist the opportunity to absorb the visual ambiguity of Buki's habiliments. Her heavy boots suggested she might have just come up from the field. Her amber hue apron was a long simply cut pinafore. The colours were soft but vivid. The dress beneath was a wine colour that irradiated the soft reds of a spring sunset. The dress didn't fall in one direction it wrapped around and tucked in. She wore a hat that followed the same deliberate disorganisation. In one sense everything about her seemed out of place, to which the reproaching glances from the librarians attested. But in another way Buki was placed perfectly, in so far as Nature should be expected to place things perfectly. Buki had all the mystique of a wondrous flower, all the presence of an ancient Oak and all the reproachfulness of an immigrant. Carmen felt the critical glare of the library staff begin to simmer into whispered disapproval, her cheeks flushed and she smoothed her dress.

Carmen hugged the books tight and gave Buki an inquisitive look. It was polite but Buki scented an accusation. She knew she was the cause of Carmen's burgeoning consternation and so, with a purposeful hand, she loosened the books from Carmen's mothering clasp and,

"My dear, you must come to my class tomorrow. I'm scared for you. You likely will kill some folk with the reckless use of them plants. I'll be doing the community a favour to teach you some proper ways."

Carmen fell hypnotically into Buki's radiance. She felt something, it might have been anticipation, it might have been a blush of liberation. With a warming smile Carmen was bewitched and Buki departed. Carmen had not given a response and eagerly wanted to know where and when the class may be held. Before she could confer Buki volunteered,

"Hall of residence by the river, tomorrow night, seven o'clock, don't be late."

With this Buki had interrupted the perpetrations of the librarians' and, with the most engaging of grins, had already begun negotiating the release of the texts.

It was after-hours and Buki was not yet a

46

member but she knew that the convictions of fate were with her and confidence ensued. Conviction also gave Carmen a fateful confidence but she chased it away with memories of hope.

10

time

Expectant mothers have cravings. Carmen had cravings but she did not expect to be a mother. She wasn't sure what she should expect. Time was the answer.

She was in desperate need of time. With my constant coming and going to lectures and meetings she could not receive the temporal latitude she needed. I was imposing upon her the habits of domestication but she needed to beat a different rhythm. I had known for sometime that I would have to provide her with opportunity but I had not expected it would come at the expense of my freedom. It was a steep price to pay but if my passage into oblivion might help her synchronise with Nature's enterprises then my evaporation would be entirely worthwhile.

11

deliverance

Madeline is French. Her gentle ways made her instantly appealing to Carmen. The two women shared the same hot plate as Buki instructed and they worked together, where possible, to solicit culinary currency. It was like gold to them, the way Buki would come by, shrewdly judge their work and validate their friendship with an inquisitive nod. They fell into a girlish bond that felt like freedom and looked like sisterhood.

Madeline had a terrible secret. She was crazy, not the most convivial of afflictions. The war had given the suffering a new bemusement known as shell-shock. This terrible intolerance left an individual incapable of making logical sense of the trauma they had endured. Some soldiers remembered the war for the friends they made and others for the friends they lost. Society sympathised with the war-weary soldier. But there were many civilians who felt unqualified to entreat the compassion of an emotionally exhausted populace and so they smothered their sadness. The resources of empathy were finite and there were many children after the war, which, imprinted with horrific and confusing experiences, were expected to simply *get-on*; Madeline was one of these.

She had endured the war as peacefully as any child might have hoped to, excepting the closing stages. She lived on a farm near a town that the war had, for the most part, ignored. It wasn't until the final Allied push that the violent reality of the conflict emerged. It was a harsh contrast. Men from every corner of the earth, it seemed, came roaring across the countryside, laying down their lives for her liberation.

Given the placid manner in which she had endured proceedings the sudden and violent means required to secure her freedom was anathematising. She wasn't aware that her freedom had been so obscured. Then for so much carnage to be executed in the name of liberation made Madeline, the child, fearful of freedom which forced Madeline, the adult, to endure a personal antithesis of liberation. Madeline had seen the mass graves, had seen the charred remains of men; had seen youth destroy youth and women weep like children.

Subsequently she had lost all sense of home. Home was a memory and England was a distraction. Buki's cooking class had been a first step, a safe step in the direction of normalcy. Carmen's friendship would be the surprise she was hoping for but her life was essentially intolerable. Madeline was the youngest in the class but was the one who felt she had the least to live for, which put an old head on her young body. She was pale and willowy, like wheat-stalk and she made Buki apprehensive. Buki wondered how a woman could be so structurally inadequate and still tolerate the rigour of kitchen work. It seemed to contradict physical laws and Buki expressed her perplexity with guarded speculation; Carmen and Madeline sympathised with giggles. Buki appreciated the frivolity at her expense. But Madeline was a farm girl and had a sound sense of her limitations.

It was strange that Madeline should choose to attend a cooking class. Food was tasteless, a consequence of sensory retraction, not uncommon among the shell-shocked, it explained her litheness. She ate what she needed and nothing more and tolerated her inability to appreciate it indifferently, pragmatically. But like Carmen she had come in search of something more than a new recipe. Likewise Buki had the intention of delivering more than cooking instruction. None were sure what they should receive from the others but they were sure they should receive it.

12

madeline and jentz

Before fleeing France Madeline had caught the attention of a German soldier. It was common for men, especially during the closing stages of the war, to be distracted by life and be subsequently prepared to turn their back on death. Many German soldiers surrendered, defected, escaped the madness with the gentle push only beauty or innocence may provide, the fall of snow, a sunrise, the turn of a dress. Jentz, frenzied with survival, encountered Madeline and in one moment his war ended.

He was seeking shelter from the fight. He no longer regarded himself as an agitator. He was a defector but had yet to consummate. He had hoped to do more than just throw his hands in the air. The barn on the farm Madeline called home was secluded and afforded him a night's invisibility. He would not have noticed it if it were not for the lantern flash and the gunfire. It was more than an hour later, once the cloud had covered, before he advanced.

There were others like him who sought to flee. They would work in teams, approach the abandoned farmhouses, seek supplies and move on. They were desperate and often disorganised. Jentz had learnt to follow in their messy footsteps. It was risky but it had allowed him to avoid various roadblocks and other traps.

He approached the farmhouse, dark and abandoned. He scampered into the adjacent barn and began frantically searching for camouflage beneath the hay. He concealed himself, considered the distant sounds of the fight and begged his ears to inform him of anything that might compromise his seclusion. He feared the Allied forces of course, but worse, he feared a fellow sympathiser, another German also seeking refuge. Deserters were dealt with in a very permanent manner and they were greatly prized, promotion and recommendations would follow. This could very quickly turn a fellow absconder into a very personal enemy. The momentum of the fight had been stung by irony.

He pulled the hay over him and listened. But the war was not concerned for his whereabouts and so he released the tension and rested. It was only then, once subtlety had returned to his senses, that he noticed her.

●　　●　　●

Madeline had become accustomed to seeking freedom in the barn. The barn was a place where Nature and the farm congregated. It was a place that was neither inside nor out. It was a place where the wonders of Nature were gently coerced to serve the needs of man. For this reason it was everything a fifteen-year-old girl should expect a shelter to be, a bastion of survival and a bosomed embrace.

Earlier that evening Madeline had been sent to the larder where the preserves were kept. It occupied a corner of the cellar. Outside the kitchen door a flight of stairs took her beneath. She would scamper, daring the darkness to dupe. It was a tripping of youth she had little opportunity to satiate. Once below the larder lamp illuminated more mature matters, responsibilities that encumbered her youth. They had lived in the dark for months. Their blackout procedures were well placed and they had created the illusion that the house had been abandoned. This evening however, as Madeline received her instructions, she took up a lantern to lead the way down the main hall and inexplicably walked out the back door.

She had turned to go down the stairs. She reached out, in the usual blind fashion, to navigate the night. *Alles ist klar*, one of only a few German phrases that she serviced, it was frivolity. But this remnant of rote from her childhood had since been made minacious. She regarded - the child she was would manage military malignancy better than the child she had become. Did God give this grace to ignorance or is Nature to blame? She skipped the first few steps and then remembered the lantern. She killed the flame. She stood motionless. Immediately she began calculating exactly how long the light had been exposed. Out the back door and turn left, down three steps - six, ten seconds? She listened for any movement. She was convinced she had brought the focus of the entire war onto the house. Silence placated but did not stop her from whispering self-admonishments. Subsequently she chastised - how could I have been so complacent and tricked into distraction by memories of a younger youth? And subsequently she felt - the war had surreptitiously disconnected her from girlhood.

Once secured beneath she relit the lantern and proceeded with her work. The cast-iron pot she used as a courier basket was heavy and battered. It had once been used to carry wood from the main kitchen fireplace to other rooms in the house. It had sat on numerous hearths and the wooden grip at the top of the handle had been burnt and was now a nest of splinters. Feeling the need to pay a penance for her lax use of the light she resolved immediately to rid the scuttle of its insidious grip. On a small workbench she proceeded to chisel at the wooden fixture. She was careful to be quiet, it made the task greater and it was some minutes later before she could break away large pieces. The last of the rotten handle fell to the floor and synchronised uncannily with a disconcerting noise above. She immediately stubbed the torch; she had learnt her lesson.

Screams, gunfire, broken glass, the mad rush of disorganised feet; heavy, panicked, then silence. She sat in the basement for an hour or longer. She would have to go to the barn. She didn't know why exactly but she felt its pull. Inside the house? Her mother and father? Dead? Prevention was the cure her mind sagely adopted and the barn's retreat would provide her ignorance with integrity. She ascended the stairs, looked out across the square of earth that she must cross and, with the nervous skip of a field mouse, found her way into the hay. It poked at her and made her itch but it was safety. Not once did she turn towards the house. She would never enter it again and the remembered warmth of its embrace would become a complicated sadness.

Her breath became still. It was the only way, given the situation, that the dust from the hay could be discouraged from affecting sneezes and coughs. She was invisible and the warmth that she needed was only just within the means of her organic enclosure to provide. The cold was teasing her and the occasional shudder was necessary. Each time the dust would pepper down and she could feel it catch in her nasal passage, a sneeze was inevitable and had never been so comprehensively attached to notions of survival. It was a miserable distraction to contemplate how a sneeze might be so deadly. She abstracted - sneezing is a symptom and a divine act so where does God begin and where does he end? She quickly put this divertissement aside and retuned to supervising her respiration.

She had become a night thing now, like the owl in the barn swooping silently on the mice. When Jentz came rushing into the space she remained motionless. Her eyes darted up, her breath stopped and she held his panicked silhouette in the centre of her vision. She was the owl watching a fleeing predator. Alarmed by its own need to be safe this predator might remain ignorant. However, he chose the same corner of the sanctuary. He approached and the owl might be forced into a fight it could not win.

● ● ●

Why the enclosure should be informed by warmth, as if anticipating his arrival, was initially beyond Jentz to infer. It was the gentle radiance of human warmth, familiar to him because, as a boy, he had shared a room with his sister. She was younger and would lie next to him on cold nights or when a storm rattled and howled. He was momentarily caused to recall her elfish smile. He was reminded that the girl he had called sister might be a survivor he will never see again.

He lay motionless and could not have known who belonged to this warmth but the lingering memory of his sister allowed him to arrest panic. He gently rolled away from his companion hoping to limit the combative options; a stout stable divider separated them. Silence prevailed. He felt alone again and considered that his companion might not be human. Farm animals have a particular way of irradiating ignorance that will cause a sleep-deprived defector to give them not a second glance. It wouldn't be the first time he had come in upon a collection of sheep or a horse. But the stillness was pervasive and much too contrived to be the cause of any domestic beast.

He crouched further back in the barn. Madeline's foot protruded from under the recess of hay he had created, a woman's leather work shoe. It was the source of the warmth and he was surprised that it had forced remembrances of his sister. Such pleasant coincidences were not consistent with the activity of war. But maybe it was no coincidence.

Since effecting his defection he had grown unusually aware - should the warmth irradiating from a woman be unique? It should! It most definitely should be!

He whispered, whistled, tapped and talked and the shoe made no response except to retreat out of the moonlight. Eventually he pulled his knife from its sheath and made an approach.

The owl had been exposed and now readied itself to be attacked. Her talons dug into her palms and she felt their dullness. The predator approached. He was armed and came forward with practiced stealth. The little owl made no sound and waited for the veil of hay to come down.

Jentz reached forward, took down the hay and exposed a girl, terrified, anticipating and beautiful. She closed her eyes defiantly and she might have been standing on the barn roof screaming her vulnerability for all to hear. He knew what she was expecting. He was a soldier, a fighter, a killer and he knew the look of expectant death; he had worn it himself. She closed her eyes. She was giving herself to death. She was giving herself to him. He felt alone again. She had given up her intelligence and made herself ready; he was led to regard her. He felt the privilege of being alone with her beauty. In that moment nothing else existed, not the stranger he had disrupted in the hay, not the war. He was alone in the quite company of her extraordinary beauty.

She opened her eyes, confusion flashed across her face and it moved him from distraction. She was not yet a woman and the war had convinced her that men were not yet worthy of her attention. But, as she considered his perplexity, her instincts activated and the little owl suddenly felt that she might yet wrangle some power to serve her needs. Survival was her immediate concern. Her instincts were her best guide and they told her to do nothing. It seemed she had cast a spell. It was beyond her ability to control but it was not beyond her to claim some advantage.

Jentz knew that she must come with him. With a change of clothes and with her as a companion his chances were better. Besides he now felt compellingly protective and the idea that he might not give her assistance could not be tolerated. In the distance he heard the fight flare and he instinctively knew that they were no longer safe. He recalled the lantern flash and the gunfire earlier. It had led him to this manger and he would not be the only respondent. He knew he must enter the house, change his clothes and seek resources. The time had come to complete his evolution from deserter to defector.

Madeline had said nothing and had not moved. She considered his peculiarities and knew that a question of survival desperately needed an answer. He knew the war; he knew how it should be evaded. His apparent, insipid avoidance of the fight told her that he was not only a coward but also determined to survive. Would it be wise? Would he be able to take her on and do more than just secure his own preservation?

It was symbiotic. She placed him on the correct side of the fight and he corrected her ignorance of the fight.

Whilst in the house he rehearsed some French phrases. His accent was not good, but if he couldn't speak? In the kitchen cupboard he found a length of cheesecloth, he tore a bandage from it. He crossed the room to where the farmer and his wife lay and, as he dipped the cloth in the blood, he regarded the kind eyes of Madeline's father. The moonlight through the smashed window made them shine but they were lifeless. He closed the lids and gave a short prayer. The bandage went around his head and forced his mouth closed. The blood would slowly leak through and give the plausible impression of a wound. He then sought some clothes from her father's collection. He pulled the shirt over his head and a vest. They dragged over the bandage and became besmeared completing the theatrics. He gave up his own knife and took a stout blade from the kitchen, heavy and worn from butchering but it was sharp. It would be his only weapon; it went into the side of his boot.

Madeline had responded to her instincts when her instincts had told her to be still, now they told her that she must move. The bare soil by the side of the barn was peppered with gravel; she heard its familiar crunch. Jentz would be coming from the house so who was this? Another deserter seeking respite? The memory of the lantern and the gunfire stung her again and she went cold - had she brought the war to bear for her sins? She retreated into the barn, sank behind a pen wall and watched from between the slats. He was slightly taller than Jentz but the silhouette of a German soldier is distinctive.

She watched him draw his side arm. Jentz turned the corner of the barn and was greeted by the commanding figure of a fellow officer. Madeline watched him balk ominously. The soldier whispered harshly at Jentz. He approached, pulled at Jentz' civilian costume and appeared to be asking many awkward questions. Jentz did not consider a response. He simply stared into the man's face apologetically and showed his hands in the fashion an unarmed man is inclined to do. The soldier lowered his gun and came very close to Jentz. The whispered exchange became less harsh; it was now a plea. He wanted a response, an answer. Jentz kept his arms by his side, his palms exposed as the soldier carefully embraced him. Madeline was reminded of an image her mother kept of Jesus addressing a wailing crowd. They too wanted answers and all he could give them was peace. Jentz did not reciprocate the embrace. The soldier stepped back and with a wilful breath regained composure. He raised the gun and forced Jentz to his knees.

Her instincts had been reasonable but now they insisted she do something that, reasonably, was unreasonable. But this night's horror had taught her that reason had very little to do with death. She stepped into the moonlight. The soldier heard the hay crack and with an expert twitch the gun found Madeline directly within its sights. Jentz also responded expertly. In one movement he produced the knife and sent the gun violently off target. The bullet pierced the barn wall and Madeline started. Jentz sent the blade deep into the man's chest. He caught his comrade as the slump of death befell and laid his loyal friend gently on the ground.

He stood and Madeline believed for a moment that she was in the company of her father's silhouette, though younger, apparently injured and now a killer. Jentz was surprised to see she had not fled, grateful that she had chosen not to abandon him and perplexed by her heroics. Time was entirely against them. He pulled his mask lose and explained that they must leave. Madeline had no functional knowledge of the German language and did nothing but stand and be still. He said in English,

"Jentz, I am Jentz."

"Madeline," she had trouble recognising the sound of her own voice.

"Very soon Madeline we will not be alone, we must leave now."

Jentz was full of reassurance but all meanings were lost on her. His words were merely sounds, incoherent, calling her to confidence like a mother bird to its fledgeling. But she was frozen, suddenly reluctant to leave the hearth of home. She looked over at the house and felt a pang of conflict. She knew it was a tomb now and could never be what she wanted it desperately to be, a time machine to reverse the night's malevolence. Detecting her confusion Jentz offered gently,

"They are at peace, they lie quite near to each other, I said a prayer."

She glared at him not sure if she should be outraged or eternally grateful. Sadness filled her heart and she began to cry. He moved towards her but she ran past him into the darkness, he followed.

His plan was simple and for that reason it would either work or they would be killed. Cross the lines, seek Allied assistance, purport to be something he was not and make his way to England. Madeline was unpredictable and he knew the time would come when she would have the chance to betray him.

Her plan was simple. Let him guide her through the jagged teeth of the frontline, appeal to the Allies, seek assurances and make her way to England. Jentz would abandon her. He would be forced to and she would let him. He had a penance to pay.

They would part and never see each other again. She resolved however, that if fate, as fate may be inclined, found some means to reunite them she would kill him. He had become her war, as close to the war as she was likely to be. He was compromised, neither good nor bad, not right nor wrong. He was everything a war needed to be and everything murder shouldn't be, neutralised. Given the chance she would seek revenge for her lost father and mother and his would be the face she'd dream of, that would keep her anger alive and keep her intentions clear.

13

the faithful

The group had been left to determine the roles and distribute the power. This organic kind of socialism was shockingly effective. The testing that took place in Dr. Richardson's rooms must have been more invasive than I was able to comprehend at the time. As crews moved around us, as the tests lead us through rigours and contemplations, as one group went about telling other groups what to do not once did I detect dissent, argument or fracturing. The cookie cutter test that we had all been subjected to, that our respective GP's had been encouraged to ply had instrumentally arranged us all into cliques, clusters and clans. This happened before we had had the chance to make acquaintances, share our first morning tea or puff a little scientific pomp.

Idleness led me to extrapolation - the roots of manipulation will easily find a footing in the putrefying pulp of hubris. I pulled the thread of the self-involved present and unveiled a draconian future where children may be assigned to a predetermined fate before they begin school. I ruminated - could the plight of an individual be secured with the manipulation of cells under a microscope? Could aptitude tests, like the one that brought these theoreticians together, be administered in utero?

The Institute was far ahead of its time. The individuals that made up its machine were not just well appointed it was destiny. It was a kind of magic, a very scientific and premeditated kind of sorcery and it was a masterful piece of manipulation. It went beyond a critical mass approach or strength of numbers. There was more to it than simply accumulating an appropriate number of like-minded individuals and hoping for the best. There was something about how these people were chosen, their propensity to be autonomous but collegiate, that made the way they were selected appear violative. It was preordained presumption.

I was one of the chosen and, without making any deliberate attempt, I became one of the chosen chosen. The six left standing were an obvious choice for no obvious reason but no one objected. I didn't feel exclusive what I felt was exclusion - could it be that my dumb standing around, while others read documents and marshalled subordinates, indicated that my genes were meant for closer examination? Where is it written by Darwin or Lamarck that inertia should be an indicator, that survival should be predicated on the tendency an individual may demonstrate to be overwhelmed and blinking?

Whatever it was that made me one of the six who should have to exist so the existence of others may be endorsed was necessarily beyond me. But I have since learnt that necessaries are not necessarily necessary. For instance, the necessary survival of a species does not necessarily coincide with the manifestation of theoretical necessaries. No, foremost, Darwinian suppositions are resolved so that chaos may find some form and distract the idle hands of redundancy. I learnt that my very important necessaries were given necessary importance because necessity for necessity's sake necessitated it. We were the tip of an iceberg buoyed by bureaucracy and the computation of our composition caused copious quantities of crimson cord to be composed. The parsimony of humanity had gone beyond the politics determined by two men in a room. It was more aligned with the sound of a room full of men clapping with one hand; invariably it becomes an orgy of backslapping.

The conviction each man and woman demonstrated in service to The Institute made me realise how capable humans are to fulfil the greatest and worst of enterprises, and why institutionalisation precipitates.

• • •

I was yet to develop a conviction and as I looked into the faces of my quarantined friends I saw confusion. I was perplexed and it may have been a moral dilemma but I could not qualify it. One week elapsed and we had given blood, been given wood block puzzles to complete with the right hand, left eye closed, then in a mirror and then blindfolded. I had completed countless miles on an exercise bike, lung capacity tested, heart rate monitored, blood pressure, hyperbaric chamber, sensory deprivation, sensory stimulation, my psychology endlessly under evaluation. Neither rhyme nor reason only a gauntlet of manipulations. We would meet most days, at the very least in passing, but our conversation was actively restricted. The first week passed and my fellow captives were still nameless.

There was method. We were surrounded by method and it kept us contained. We were scientists and we knew that an experiment's subjects must not be biased. We might have had four or six words together throughout the course of a day otherwise we dutifully complied with the regulations. However, after six days or so our brief exchanges had become infused with subtleties, a wry smile, a wink. Like the persecuted making fish marks in the sand we were encouraging encoded elucidations.

We were separated from the community by curtains much like a hospital ward. The commotion of scientific happenings circled around us but we had no intelligence. For a week we had been cocooned in a prison of veils. We followed directions and went blindly along. Abruptly that changed.

On the morning of the seventh day I was given a uniform of sorts. I was happy to put aside the white hospital garb. The blue pants were utilitarian and the white shirt was crisp and fitted. The cubical chair by the bed was moved forward. I was sitting at the foot of the bed facing the fourth-wall curtain of my little space when the temporary nature of our confines was violently laid bare. The curtains flew away, beds were banished, everything wheeled into recesses and a large table landed in the centre of the space. Disorientation dissolved and our new arrangements came into focus. We sat in a perfect circle around the table separated from the next person by six or seven feet. Without the need to make a physical contribution we had been corralled into, what was effectively, a common area.

He had been invisible to us for the duration but now the American with the eyepatch appeared. It was not without some orchestration of course. The personnel synchronised their exit, the curtained walls of our new enclosure acknowledged their departure with a ripple and then silence, absolute. Suddenly there was no intelligible commotion, no hubbub of movement. The technicians, the assessors, the laboratories, beyond our observation but always in motion, were still, dragooned by Dulaney. Anticipation simmered into awkwardness as the silence stretched. One of us, I do not recall who, opened their mouth but said nothing.

14

dulaney

Dulaney stood with hands in pockets, head down. He always appeared to have more pressing cogitations to cogitate. His gait suggested a predatory disposition. He stood at the edge of our circle; there was no eye contact. His inertia endured but the group held its silence. Eventually the discomfort subsided, the silence persisted but it became defined by something else, reverence.

It occurred to me, at that moment, silence is intolerable. Humans are opposed to its insidiousness. Silence is truth because it forces us into the company of the liar *procreation* requires us to manifest. Self must lie because life must push against something to stimulate continuance. Social negotiations are lies that force life to endlessly manoeuvre its energy. To be silent is to commune with that energy. We are a compromised demonstration of its potential. The universe hopes that we should become that energy entirely and no longer be the liar, which is the purpose of death. Silence therefore, answers the question, does life have purpose? Yes, to love the lie and die.

He spoke to us in a cool but cautious manner from behind his tailored, black leather eyepatch and instantly I felt I could not trust him. In my estimation his hidden peeper was portraying the paradigms of perjury. The eyepatch and a stayed manner combined to exaggerate his aloofness. However, the relaxed but direct way in which he spoke had an endearing quality. It was a combination that had the ability to manipulate you into doing the kind of things you would have no one to blame but yourself for doing. The Institute needed a man like this. I would soon discover the opposite was truer. He needed the insulating effect of a secret organisation. He required The Institute to nurture the madness he was masquerading as aggressive science.

If the Americans were involved that meant the fear that motivated The Institute's initiatives must have been either very real, or very much imagined to be more than real. His surveillance of us was subtle, but with every twitch of his eye he took in another detail and I felt naked.

"Welcome," he started, "I am Dulaney, United States Military Intelligence. The formative stages of this program are now complete. The results are most impressive and The Institute greatly appreciates your ongoing participation."

He began to circle the table still reluctant to make sustained eye contact. He continued,

"Soon the next phase will begin. You will start by building relationships, unique bonds. This will facilitate the clinical aspect of the study."

Clinical aspect? Had we not been thoroughly, completely, entirely, clinically determined, assessed, devised and contorted? What more would we be expected to endure clinically?

He continued,

"I will oversee the next phase personally and the course that you take from this juncture will be entirely a consequence of my command. It is important that you understand this."

He made no attempt to conceal an ominous implication. We choreographed a twitching of eyebrows that I felt confirmed a mutual foreboding. The last stop before destiny was being called and those with any reservations please mind-the-gap. Dulaney paused to allow the semaphore of uneasiness to circulate. Happy that we understood he went on,

"It is reasonable to say that the true work lies ahead of you. Soon you will be transported to a top-secret military site code named *The Facility*. Consider everything so far as a target acquisition exercise. Now? We pull the trigger."

His one eye targeted each one of us in turn and in the same undeterred manner in which he entered, he exited.

We now had our chance to form understandings. The commotion of The Institute beyond the paper walls of our enclosure resumed. For a week we had been directed, paraded, partitioned, escorted and chaperoned. Now? We were mystified by our newly acquired autonomy. Names? Professions? Origins? We were a room full of adults gifted with numerous social skills that, with the interference of one week's befuddlement, had been disabled.

Another unreasonable silence endured until the arrogance of its dumb intrusion could no longer be entertained. He was tall, an athlete, intimidating but coy and he spoke correctly. His thick blond hair and burnt complexion told me something about his pursuits,

"Non sibi sed patriae?"

The first sound to emanate from within our new coven, it was disorientating. His manner was soft and contradicted his muscular form. His name was Michael. The silence had been broken; anticipation asked, who next?

"Ante faciem domini."

His name was William and he produced this adjunct as a reflex. He was shorter, wore glasses and with the addition of a lab coat he might have been a humbled technician. He might have been an infiltrator, taken from the ranks of subordinates but his bearing was astute and unaffected.

"I feel like my brains have been out for a week."

Her name was Anna, tall, short red hair, Scottish, an odd gangly creature prone to sighs and putting her face in her hands. She spoke in a lazy manner but deliberately giving the impression that she might be sagacious. It was not misleading. Through the course of coming turmoils Anna said many right things at the right time.

"Time has been, that, when the brains were

out, the man would die, and there an end."

This was my contribution and it afforded me happy memories of Carmen. She would have feigned bemusement. She knew my allusions were limited to Shakespeare.

Jane said nothing for Jane had nothing to say. Jane was a coordinator, self-appointed. For the duration this matronly pragmatic woman was inclined to only say things that were necessary and immediately concerned with the business of organisation.

Miriam was also taciturn but this was her default state. She remained aloof with such consistency that I regarded her as genuinely enigmatic. Her reticence might have been interpreted as rudeness. But she presented what she was for all that it was and it was lacunal, an urn wanting graffiti. Soon she would be compelled to contemplate the bearing of my child.

Much can be said with sayings of nothing and we had just catalogued a modest array of nothings. The conversation began to flow eventually, and we learnt about our histories, education, specialities, likes, dislikes, wants, needs, impressions and there were no surprises. We were a collection of *above-averagers*.

Behind everything we postured however, was the desire to understand. What was the purpose? Who were the benefactors? What should we be required to do next? We felt exposed; the walls were thin. Beyond our isolation, only inches beyond the boundary of our enclosure, The Institute persisted with its distractions. It was more than reasonable to assume we were being monitored, every word.

We examined the peculiarities of our new arrangements. There were separate sleeping quarters for men and women, a communal area, a small preparation space with burner, refrigeration, sink, pantry and perishables. The beds were now adorned with a footlocker containing essentials.

Observed, assessed and placated. But we had been given some command of our destiny now. Unity was expected but we expected to demonstrate it in our own time and manner. Not that we coordinated to do so. It started as a silence indicative of our initiation. For a week we had been isolated, corralled, contained like animals, a few words shared and we owed those responsible nothing. Silence was our rebellion.

But we had learnt the language of gesture. With looks and subtleties we had learnt to share and respond. Without the need for it to be formally established this now became our preferred means of communication. We were being clever, denying the establishment the pleasure of our data. Not that we had the need to discuss anything. There were no tasks, no directives just an allocation of time to be done with what-we-will. Another week I expected, a week of silent confinement, I was correct.

● ● ●

The seven days expired without interruption, with one exception. Silence seemed to seep like vapour from our curtained chamber and infect the entire building. After three or four days all was quiet. Our mute rebellion began to feel invalid without the counterpoint of other commotion. One afternoon I decided to step beyond the walls of the enclosure and into exposure.

It was empty. The entire building was cleared, a frigate, hangers full of bombers, a dozen trains with locomotives, fleets of busses could easily be catered for. Our small piece of territory sat like a blight within the hollowed arena. In the distance a door jared open and a lab coat came purposefully towards me. Minutes passed as I stood and watched the messenger make her long approach,

"Please come with me."

I obliged. Now the long march back to the door, like a mouse hole, like an Alice door in the side of a massive rabbit hole. It opened into a decommissioned control room with disused instruments and missing panels. Through to a passage, small square windows down one side, tessellated. The blinds were drawn. Through a door to the right between the glass, a table, one chair, I was alone. The far wall had a row of windows beyond arms reach and provided a view of the bleak sky beyond.

"Take a seat, if you like."

Dulaney had materialised behind me. He was shrouded in a grey mood consistent with confinement. I slid my hands into my pockets, remained erect and silent. He smiled,

"You are right to be curious," he countered as he closed the door and assumed a lean.

His pallid qualities were noteworthy. His

symptoms were indicative, exhaustion. I was compelled to ponder - in what way had the benign business of the last few days contributed to his fatigue. Then came purpose - there were answers that needed questioning and this was my chance. What had we been expected to achieve with the passing of these few days? Were we required to pursue an understanding? We had been given no notion of what was and why it should be.

The ideas formed, I opened my mouth, I closed it again, I looked at him and he said nothing, silence. Questions were not the answer; time was the answer. Dulaney knew this better than I could hope to at the time,

"The next phase will soon begin. Your progress is exemplary and your continued patience appreciated."

In response I said nothing. He clicked the door open. But before inviting me to exit he postured,

"Which do you fear more, that history might repeat itself, or that it might not repeat itself?"

"Both," my reply earned me a smile, a laugh almost.

The technician returned and I retreated back down the hall, Dulaney watched.

The welcoming committee anticipated my return and congregated accordingly. We stood beyond the flimsy walls of our enclosure, admired the colossal space and I responded to the query of expressions with a shrug and,

"The next phase begins soon, I am not sure entirely what that might involve, but our on going participation is appreciated."

Will stepped into the space,

"So, we must pass the time the best we can."

Players, teams, bowler, batter all very quickly arranged. The apparatus was made with the ingenious use of found-items. The bat had been fashioned from a slat taken from Michael's footlocker. The ball was secured by dissecting one of the casters supporting the main table. It was hard and plastic and slightly too small. It rebounded off the cement unpredictably and we all responded heartily to the danger it posed.

We would cycle through in order, each of us swinging with mad abandon, determined to discover if the limits of this oversized cell could be reached. The smooth ball flew with astonishing speed and put us all on edge. Michael could bowl fast. He was strong and skilled. We all stood in line to face him. It was David and Goliath. He would bear down with all his speed. The ball would descend from a height of ten feet or more. The garbage can we used as wickets suffered. No one could hit him. The ball would smash into the can, the appeal would go up and everyone would celebrate another fallen gladiator. Michael would laugh and blush. When on the attack he could be relied upon, it was reassuring.

Will was the only one to claim the kill zone. The ball was high, a sharp pull and it would soar across the arena. The magnitude of the establishment made boundaries almost inconceivable. Will was determined, however, to exploit Michael's pace and send the ball into orbit if possible. He was too slow.

The ball hit him in the chest, full and hard. He dropped the bat, hopped about, clutching and massaging, he moaned and laughed. He was in pain but he was brave. I faced a lethal ball, it split me in two and left a hole in the tin bin. Anna got close. She let one go through, weighed it up and steadied for the next salvo. Jane had been a softball catcher so she stood as wicketkeeper and took the ball well back with a clamshell like clasp effectively, she was fearless. The next ball came. It bounced high. From where I stood it came straight for Anna's head. She moved an inch to avoid the concussion. She raised the bat, indicative of baseball and showed the face. The ball glanced and went racing off over Jane's head. It was unorthodox but there was contact and it was skilful. Jane chased the ball down a few feet from the boundary.

Miriam stepped forward. She held the bat assuredly. She might never have played before but that wasn't going to stop her from parading confidence. Michael sensed the challenge and Miriam wanted a full taste of the danger. She could not be regarded any way other than most seriously. She managed to infuse everything she did with a sense of necessity. The game suddenly became a test of nerves and reflexes, resolve and conviction. Michael paced in and threw his arm up violently. I could not make out the flight. The ball hit short I presume, Miriam swung and, contact. It was middle and cut straight across the face. We all watched the small white beacon sail. It cleared the outfield, went over my head and kept rocketing.

We hadn't noticed him, Dulaney, it was stealth, a habit of war, a survivalist's disposition. Smash! The ball penetrated a far window. It was high and the glass rained down after a pause of several seconds, the cavern retarded time. We all turned and pointed our amazement at Miriam eager to see her reaction. But she had caught his eye. Dulaney retreated into the common area, Miriam followed accordingly and, having felt the cooling effect of the creepy American, we all fell in line.

"In the next few days," he began, "you will be relocated. To facilitate this move you will be paired."

He paused. He wanted the resonance of the word *paired* to penetrate,

"This coupling will be summative. It will form the basis of the final phase."

He paused again. We were silent. He allowed a spurious tension to build and inform our need for assurance. He was a master manipulator and knew the seeds of coercion often need pungent silences to sprout. The pauses were pregnant and the irony was suffocating. He continued,

"The frontline of war shall be redefined. With your intervention the future of conflict will evolve. War is a struggle between strengths, between the strongest of the strongest, the fittest of the fittest. Modern conflict will be evinced once the distillate of humanity is appropriated."

I thought of God again. I saw myself reach out and touch his face. Craggy, pitted, cratered, ice and eternal, it told the story of creations endless helix. I was sobered by the prospect of new life, of a designed existence, of paternity, the influence of society and environment.

He paused again. He lingered in a style that demanded our obedience. I had never met a man who could make such talented and varied use of peace. He had thrown a blanket of unity over us, a oneness of scientific mentality. We had known this moment would come, the moment when potential must become action and action must be procreation.

"Clinically," he said, "everything has been done to ensure your contribution is viable. It began with you, it has all been because of you and it will end with you and with what you must do next."

I mused - the beasts are being called into the ark two by two and then the flood. The comparison was stratified with uncertainty - should life as we know it be refocused by speculative Adams and reluctant Eves? It was clear that I was not the only one to feel the flex of fate or to taste the bittersweetness of Dulaney's unscrupulous science. But we were essentially, preoccupied with anticipating who might be expected to combine with whom.

Dulaney paused again to admire the awkwardness, to delight I assume, in our human propensity to seek comfort in assumption. We were not disappointed. Michael would be asked to match his physical perfection with Jane's tendency to be very well organised. Their offspring would be a leader of Adonis proportions. Will and Anna would produce a genius with a considered approach, a quiet achiever, an old-soul type. Miriam and I were expected to conjoin. What would be our contribution? The commentator and the clinician? A child blessed with introspection and driven by empiricism? The ingredients for a consummate science-fictionalist or a committed fictional scientist; like father, like child?

What proved to be the most unusual aspect of the proposition was the manner in which Dulaney communicated the arrangements. He concluded,

"Time will measure you. Interminable units of immortality shall frame your anthropological symmetry. But you must enter this next phase boldly. The fruits of your labour shall endure, this is my assurance to you."

He then produced a set of exquisite botany and entomology renderings. They were housed in a folded card adorned with a gold embossed skeletal representation of a leaf. The rendering inside the card was an original ink and watercolour design of the most extraordinary tropical plants and insects. The colours and finery made the images appear to move.

The cards were paired. He was positioned under the hooded entrance of our cloth bunker. He called Michael and Jane forward and, imposed by specious ceremony, they approached the improvised altar. The men received the insect drawing and the women received the flower.

Dulaney brought each couple in close and whispered. Miriam and I were informed that the bee, which had been gloriously represented on my card, a blue bee with a vivid sheen and a solid frame, takes nectar from an orchid. Miriam's orchid depended upon my bee. Its heavy hood and recessed anatomy could only be accessed by the determined efforts of my specific type of bee.

It was a strange kind of consummation. Why he chose to bring us into our unions in such a bewildering manner was initially beyond my comprehension. I later realised we were being bamboozled intentionally. We sat down as couples with our decorative documents perplexed. The many queries we could have constructed were cancelled by confusion. What about the nurturing? Were we expected to give our child up entirely? Is the female expected to endure the pregnancy phase alone? What about institutionalisation? Alienation? What about baptism and God? Do we give the child a name? We had been hoodwinked. These questions and many others like them went wanting. We allowed Dulaney to retreat unhindered, unquestioned and it would be the last we saw of him for yet another week.

15

pilgrims

Buki held two classes in the first week, Carmen and Madeline attended both. She was only mildly surprised to see them attend the second class. They had become fast friends or second sisters and Buki had become their spiritual surrogate. Buki knew very well the forces they were responding to, the churn of change. It was palpable. Two women in desperate need of liberation and they had found each other. They were grateful to Buki; the Tuesday night class had been a revelation.

Madeline suggested that they attend Thursday night also and that she might come past Carmen's house and they might go together. She had blurted it out on the Tuesday night in a moment of distraction amid messy kitchen activity. Carmen was checked; Madeline was caught and felt rejection take aim. Carmen responded with an instinctual turn of reassurance. She took Madeline's hand,

"Come by at six, I have a tea drying, from my garden, we'll have a cup and make our way."

With that the friendship was consummated.

Tears fell on to the knife and the blade blurred. Madeline lifted her apron and dabbed. The onions hissed across the oily surface of the pan as Buki sagely noted the interaction; she kept a watchful distance.

Madeline lamented - how is it that I should fear a step towards friendship? Why is it that I should doubt the connection? Is it fraudulent that I should be sure of our bond but fearful of its demonstration? No, the survival instinct will not tolerate displays of weakness. I can feel, free of fear, but expression draws attention. I am then exposed and vulnerability succeeds. She philosophised - friendship needs risk otherwise trust will not germinate.

Carmen had felt something come alive within. But was it more than reciprocating Madeline's small steps towards rebirth? Accordingly, she had given Carmen something maternal. Buki was the matriarch, a Godmother figure but Carmen was the nurturer Madeline needed. In many ways Madeline was still a girl, war-wrecked but juvenile. It is a curious combination that places innocence next to resilience, spring next to autumn and creates a conundrum, what should youth see through the eyes of the dead? She needed to transition from weathered bud into reborn bloom and Carmen felt, instinctually, that she should be the one to facilitate it.

The Thursday class ended, Madeline and Carmen were the last to leave and Buki stopped them at the door,

"Fast friends you have become, this makes

Buki very happy. Though Madeline you need to be a sister in more than passion only. Give your body some greater care and eat."

Madeline retorted,

"I've had two good meals this week, I've not taken such care for a long time."

Buki accepted the compliment and took the opportunity,

"You must come this Sunday, it will be the solstice and there is something special I have prepared. Meet me here just after sunset."

Buki had given a command and the two women could not begin to imagine how she might be refused. They were willing participants and they skipped into the darkness arm in arm, filled with girlish delight.

Sunday was now an eagerly anticipated adventure. On the way home Madeline spoke the praises of Carmen's homegrown tea and Carmen insisted that they stop and have some more. The two women entertained another two hours of conversation with the assistance of the tea. Carmen heard about the war, the farm and a mysterious German soldier and Madeline's escape. Carmen listened as Madeline talked about the anger she harboured and the lingering sadness.

Carmen observed however, that the vehement hatred that should accompany such anger seemed checked; she said nothing. Madeline felt something similar. She no longer recalled the hate quite so immediately. Had ten years passed meant her passions should wane? By sharing with Carmen was she freeing herself of the tumult? She forcefully recalled her resolution and once again Jentz' face was the image of death she betokened.

Carmen was led into a cheeky divergence; she indulged a pause then,

"How would you do it?"

"How would I do what?" Madeline cautioned.

"This German, the deserter, if you saw him again, how would you…"

"Kill him?" Madeline obliged.

"Yes," Carmen's eyes were alive with mischief.

Madeline wasn't certain how it might be done. She wasn't expecting it ever to be done. But she could see that the idea of it had given Carmen's fancy considerable flight and so she mused sympathetically.

Carmen stood, took Madeline by the hand and led her through the cloakroom and into the garden. It was dark and Madeline relied on Carmen's eager guidance. The moonlight gave the outline of the small wooden shed a pearlescent quality and Madeline was taken by a girlish sense of adventure, she giggled and tripped. Carmen pulled a lantern from an old fruit box and struck a match. Aware of the inherent drama, she lifted the flame and filled her face with ominous shadows,

"What I am about to reveal will give you power over life and death, invisible death. It will make you see Nature for the mother of mischief she is. *O, mickle is the powerful grace that lies*
In plants, herbs, stones, and their true qualities;

For naught so vile that on the earth doth live
But to the earth some special good doth give;
Nor aught so good but, strain'd from that fair use,
Revolts from true birth, stumbling on abuse."

Carmen gave a mocking rendition of this Romeo and Juliet. She turned her eyes up and placed the flame at an acute angle. Madeline found the effect most ghoulish. The hairs on her arms tingled with anticipation. Carmen crept into the room and Madeline followed mimicking her Machiavellian manner.

The lantern swung from a central hook and Carmen made the flame strong. Madeline saw the drying shelves full of uprooted stalks with their soil-encrusted ends. Some plants were greenish, others had yellowed and some had purpled. Some still held onto small flowers and others were nothing more than blackened, leathery husks. The bench at the far end where mortar and pestle, knives and blocks, tins and beakers were arranged was stained and gouged.

Madeline's senses expanded and consumed the perfume. She was on the farm again. Fresh hay, trodden grass, livestock, summer rain, yeast, cinnamon and her mother's scented soap. She had been anaesthetised. For ten years her senses had been ignorant. Buki's cooking class, Carmen's tea and now this potent atmosphere had given life back to her sensibilities.

She became momentarily drunk on the cocktail of fumes and memories. But then the complexities emerged and she identified a familiar tea aroma. Many other tastes were familiar and some had a

87

strange and possibly offending quality. Carmen admired Madeline's stunned appraisal and the way she greedily fed on the life giving vapour. It led her to contemplate - how is it that this plant mortuary should be so affirming? How is it that Nature can be so potently contradictory? She concluded - energy is constant, Nature is cyclic and so death is life.

Carmen interrupted the meditation by retrieving a hand-full of dried leaves from a canister. She opened Madeline's hand and filled her palm. There was a row of containers that sat on a shelf near the door filled with various teas. Madeline instantly recognised that evening's suppertime delight. Next, Carmen retrieved a vial. It came from an apothecary case, antiquated but functional and well hidden under the workbench. There were many small identical bottles from which Carmen chose carefully. She uncorked the slender mouth. In her left hand Madeline now held the tea and in her right a small glass bottle filled with hoary, spiked flakes. She raised the bottle to her nose but Carmen caught her hand. She then closed the leaves into her fist. She held Madeline firm and fixed her gaze.

Madeline felt the frivolity evaporate. Carmen held her attention entirely. She put pressure on Madeline's left hand and the leaves disintegrated,

"These juiced flowers, give life."

She gestured the vial. Madeline's knuckles had whitened around the tiny flask and Carmen added,

"With these nettled flakes? It is taken."

She released Madeline, took back the bottle and returned to the case. Madeline reeled. Fantasy lifted her as she arrested images of Jentz. She could see his lips curving around the cup's edge, the poison supped, its wickedness beginning to work and his eyes rolling back, convulsions and then suffocation.

She had sought a means. Unknowingly, subconsciously, she had been longing for a means and now she had it. It was a marriage of ideals. With Nature's nudge she could take back her memories entirely, she could languish eternal, let her youth return again to that place where Mother-earth begs to nurture. But she would never be given the opportunity. The symbolic Jentz, possibly dead, would unlikely ever materialise. But if fate should allow for the impossible blessed Nature had delivered a means.

●　　●　　●

Buki sat waiting for midnight. The garden had been turned, the soil was warm with the activity of composting and the moon languished. This was a witching time and she reflected on forgotten notions of mystery. The Middle Ages had made a silly mess of it all. It was a time when witch-hunts were tools politicians deployed to lever control. Today humans suffer from an over excited understanding of containment. She mused - nothing has changed because nothing has changed. Nature's force will guide us. We might make small changes to our course but nothing will come of ostentation and Nature will not be restrained. Accept that there is art in action but be small in the face of Nature and you shall be embraced by the energy of an entire planet.

She marvelled at the trickery of science and the beguiling of witchcraft. She proposed - when curiosity taunts conviction subsides and when it whispers conviction revives. She thought of the coming solstice and the two women from her class, she felt the worth of her influence. She would take them into Nature, into a cosmic midnight and revel to them that of themselves, which they yet know not of. She then thought of Shakespeare and a young African, Achebe, he might write a book one day.

16

exile

He would never forget the love this foreign home had afforded him. Or the strange encounter with a beautiful girl named Madeline that made his rebirth possible. He had put her on a boat to England and she stood, statuesque on its stern, apparently unmoved and the ship cleared. He spent the next eight months attending to the medical needs of Allied soldiers. Once behind the lines his skills were desperately required.

●   ●   ●

He had been marshalled with Madeline into a line of civilians. The encampment was close to the fighting and organised chaos had supervened. Some very awkward questions were about to be put to him. The bandage around his head would be forcibly removed and suspicions would be aroused. They shuffled along, he slowly began to remove the bandage. He gave Madeline a fateful glance. He had fulfilled his obligation to her. He had his penance to pay and she had delivered him to a bloodied altar.

The large red cross on the side of a truck raced

past and stopped nearby. The rush came from all directions. Jentz gave Madeline's hand a squeeze, their eyes met and he melted into the bloody throng. He found a man with shrapnel in his leg; he was dying. Jentz clutched the limb and the bleeding eased. It bought him access into the main medical tent. For the next nine months he continued to clasp the haemorrhages and betray his homeland.

●   ●   ●

England was his home now. For ten years he had continued his medical studies. He had been acknowledged for his research. Together, Behavioural Science and Genetics might form a new frontier. Ironically his German origins garnered him some unexpected kudos. His work was a secret, a government secret and so was his existence.

Days spent in the recesses of Oxford University processing candidates, refining the techniques and performing a myriad of preparatory tasks. The Institute had developed an impenetrable system of secrecy. Discovering how it might be compromised caused him to stretch his imagination beyond limits. If he were to reveal the small piece of the puzzle to which he was privy what reaction might it attract? It would expose him as a lunatic. His would be a lonely voice of madness talking about things that science-fiction writers were hesitant to conjure.

●   ●   ●

I was the exception, Dr. Mathewson, a title given to me courteously. Beyond the walls of the

University I was known as author John Mathewson. But an author of what? Jentz would ruminate - Pseudo-science pseudo-fiction? He had caught site of me wandering the University halls and it made him regard how unimpressive the utterly impressive might be when they are occupied in the unimpressive business of complacency. It occurred to him that Universities were often very effective at putting academics and their potential to sleep. He was astute. My academia was the friend the establishment kept close but my potential was the enemy they kept a much closer eye on.

He was uncertainly a follower. Was my work factual fantasy or plausible pulp? The ambitions were off the map but he enjoyed how I satirically navigated empiricism towards its jaded ambitions. Jentz appreciated the intoxication of my contradictions. Ultimately, he idealised the Dr. John I had reluctantly become, as many were inclined to do, and harboured a secret ambition to convert my fiction into fact. The Institute gave him the opportunity.

He would be momentarily surprised when, some time later, he would see me occupying a bed at The Institute. I cannot recall having seen him but Jentz believed that if The Institute owed immortality to anyone it would surely be me. I would have been inclined to agree.

● ● ●

He was relocated to Oxford for a total of three months, which included two weeks in London. He then planned to return to Buckinghamshire. His

93

psychiatry practice and research would continue and the clandestine operations of The Institute would become a potent memory.

•   •   •

Upon completing his contracted time in London The Institute decamped. As he left the massive enclosure for the last time the outpost of sheeted fences, which housed my compatriots and me, appeared significantly marginalised. He was the outsider, a German and yet he felt we were the refugees that he must regard empathetically.

He returned to Oxford, to his seclusion from exclusion. He might have regarded the entire affair as a holiday of sorts if it were not for the loneliness. Men are meant to fight but a man is not a fighter until he fights and then he can be little else. Jentz had given of himself to be cleansed of his sins, time, blood, tears and guilt. Still the dead would let linger their melancholy and he was hounded. Sleepless nights spent answering their call with shouts and fits. Morphine was not a cure but it allowed him to close his eyes and see only blackness.

Essentially, he was a liar and he had come to a crossroads. He had spent ten years asking for forgiveness for doing something he couldn't admit to, it was futile. He was nineteen when he made his emancipation. He would consider how he and the strange girl in the barn must have appeared very fresh faced as they pioneered a path to freedom. He challenged - how reasonable is it that I cling to the guilt? My younger self must be commended not disrespected with fateful admonishments. He had

94

chosen not to serve evil and killed a comrade in the process. He had freed a vulnerable girl. Jentz recalled her beauty. Her memory was a respite amongst a catalogue of scientific contemplations. The image of her was an oasis.

The past would never abandon him but it might be encouraged to walk behind and not constantly by his side. How he should attend this was beyond his reckoning, except that something as fateful as a war was surely the only means to interrupt recollections of a war.

17

go forth

I am given to recall a hesitant moment I shared with Carmen that now infuses my memories with the distinctive essence of irony. Before any of the madness had evolved, before the truth had become just another obscurity, on the very day of my first assessment, compliments of Dr. Richardson, I stood inside the front door of our home and considered my first lie. I assumed it would cut too close to make associations between her fertility and my genetic potential; I discerned. Paranoia could easily have convinced her that science might make use of my genetic material more assuredly than she could ever hope to. Science was forcing me to betray the woman I love and what might I pay for the privilege? An illegitimate child who will have a lifetime of institutionalisation to appreciate?

Science would have its chance to make good use of my genetic material but it would not be the clinical endeavour I had expected. It wasn't even love in a test tube. It would seem that after science has said everything it can about experimental

96

conditions, controlled environments and artificial mechanisms there is no substitution of parsimony. Science requires two humans to come together and do what comes naturally or in this instance, unnaturally naturally.

Miriam would be my partner in this unholy consummation. Her mind and bearing were seemingly unchangeable. She was a piece of geology waiting on the shore of enlightenment to be examined very scientifically. She was thoroughly biased and influenced by an observer effect. She seemed to behave in a manner that assumed she was under constant appraisal. Not that she craved approval. It was more that her entire being had come about purely to facilitate scientific observation. She was a laboratory fixture with all the sex appeal of a petri-dish and she was everything science-fiction dreams are made of.

I wasn't entirely sure why it had to be executed in accordance with Nature's means. It had been explained that hormone levels and other chemical responses are observable and therefore natural conception is preferred. But was it mandated? Was it an absolute? Were there other means? Was it hubris? Am I God? In small degrees we had been led away from the noble pursuit and recruited into divine demonstrations. But we were rude animals playing with the tools of creation and we had no intelligence. What would be the true violence of this act? What mess would we make of Nature's order?

I entertained much philosophical fretting in my attempt to avoid certain certainties. I was not likely to compromise the entire initiative by insisting that some other means be made available. Either I accepted the moral consequences of sexual intercourse with Miriam or I returned to Oxford and let the future of the species be determined without my hallowed contribution. Would my non-participation dilute the outcome? Compromise the curve? Pollute the purpose? Would my credibility be traumatised? Would I be left to splash superfluously about in some little pond of science-fiction and surrender all scientific kudos? Would the likes of Miriam ever be likely again to acknowledge my peerage? And another layer of latent resentment would be left to tarnish domesticity. I could never let Carmen know what was motivating my damaged sense of purpose and, in the quiet manner to which she had become accustomed, would be left to blame herself.

Miriam surely did not give the bigger picture a moment's introspection. The miniature circle of light cast upon the stage of creation projected by a microscope was the only theatre of objectivity Miriam patronised. She efficiently consigned the demonstrations of man to an anthropological pragmatism. We are sophistic entities brought into being by the desire to demonstrate. The microscope looks at the raw ingredients and Miriam marvelled at the phenomenon - at what point in the assembly of these micro-makings did humans become so intolerably demonstrative?

She came from a dehumanised position, a clinician's ivory tower from where she could distribute the forces of *why*. Scientists are the masters of component-ism and *why* is the gravity that pulls the components together and forms something greater. Miriam was the gravity, an uncompromisable force or so I thought.

There were three buses. They each had blackened windows, a military police escort and a driver. We boarded, one bus per couple, we never saw The Institute's external aspect. We travelled for an hour or more beyond the city. Gravel ricocheted off the wheel arches and the countryside scented the cabin. The army owns land, a small country within a country and we were immigrants.

18

the facility

The establishment was purposeful. There was nothing fabricated, nothing temporary. The Facility was a bastion of scientific and military prowess. Delightfully futuristic and I felt entirely at home. Stark, clean, secure, hidden, it was a lair. It was plucked from my imagination and I was caused to consider the future less whimsically than I was accustomed to. It had arrived and I was knocking on its door.

Military police managed the entrance. Beyond the first set of security doors the sharp figure of a warrior stood. He was a soldier, a powerhouse of astute muscularity. His civilian suit did little to conceal the true nature of his combative means. We were ushered forward. The doors closed behind us. He considered us indifferently. The phone on his desk rang. It was loud and I was startled, Miriam did not flinch. He let it ring a few times, his focus fixed on us. Without corrupting his eye's commitment to our containment the receiver found his ear. He seemed unbreakable. Eventually, Miriam and her vacant forces beat his stare. He said nothing and returned the receiver to its cradle, proceeded to the doors and pushed them open. Before us lay a village of underground pretensions.

The inhabitants of this village all wore the same white lab coats, all murmured the same white lab coat language and all carried the same white lab coat paraphernalia such as clipboards. The heavy work was wrought by drudges wearing white overalls and hairnets. They came and went through a door at one end and I caught glimpses of a blue room. To my left sat controllers at panels and at instruments with pens and papers. We were ushered to the left and disappeared into a corridor with apparently endless avenues.

We were shown a room, a table, two chairs. I sat, Miriam took a guarded position against the wall and we shared a look, protracted, nothing to be said. Anything we said would expose a horrible truth, a truth that ends with science but begins with an intimate fiction. I closed my eyes, Carmen?

It had been two weeks. It had been time enough for everything to change; mendacious memories malign. One more week and we would be together again. This experience had affected me or at the very least, had left a blemish on my habitude that I would find difficult to conceal. Would it inform our reunion? Would it mar the future? Would she be the woman I love or the woman she has longed to be and might they be the same person?

19

solstice

Buki let the night's glow glance her face. Her two companions crept along behind hugging arms and whispering giggles. Buki moved them away from the town's illumination. The ground grew soft, the coolness enclosed, the ripples of the river echoed gently. The two friends became quiet. The stillness of the forest now demanded their attention.

Buki allowed the familiar sense of enchantment to enshroud her, putting to sleep the restlessness of the day's distractions. The darkness was all around, interposed by a magnesium lustre. Buki meditated - the moon is sister, friend, daughter, mother, a silvery servant and she exposes Nature for what it truly is, a place of concealment. The sun is father, son, creator and he looks with the penetration of X-rays. He is fooled into thinking his intelligence is complete. It is the moon however, that coaxes and rejuvenates. In the rich thickness of night life finds purpose in meditation and dreams correct our meaning.

Carmen and Madeline had given up their

girlish entwining and began to feel the sway of Buki's metamorphosis. They circled around her, mesmerised by suffusing stillness and the alertness of their senses. Buki struck a flint and the fire pit flicked with flame; it was soon a blaze.

They stood in a circle around the glow, wide-eyed and vacant. Buki had instigated this expedition, she had let the journey be the means and now neutrality possessed them. No magic words, no poetry or song, just the haunting whisper of the night and the dancing of the flame. Their glassy gaze, their entranced dedication to the illumination would have put the most assured night stroller or beating Bobby back on their heels. The uninformed intensity of their distraction was impenetrable and Buki knew it was time.

20

temptation

The technician, like a nurse or a midwife, entered the room. I was about to engage Miriam in conversation, I was about to make the silence awkward, I was about to let the elephant in the room roar, I was saved. She deposited two sets of clothes, unisex, formless, underwear included. She exited and the silence persisted. Then Miriam began to loosen the buttons on her shirt. I stood and released the shirt from my pants. Nakedness approached and with it the manifestation of rude potentials and so I let a distraction defuse - numerous changes of clothing styles had been required recently. *Scientifique-couture* is informed with more variety than I would have previously assumed.

Nakedness had arrived, almost. Clad only in her underthings she stepped into the light and gathered up a formless brassiere for analysis. Indecision brought forth more silence. Then abruptly she removed the remainder of her clothes, stood before me defiant, completely naked, allowed me to consider her details and then she dressed. She was perfect. Science could not have intentionally rendered a female better formed. In terms of proportion she was everything a seductress could be, a mother should be, a companion desires and lust might invent. I was astonished. I removed the remainder of my clothes and she threw me a glance. It was a reflex and all the attention my details demanded, apparently.

The courtship was over, the ice broken. Consummation had endured its introductory phase and I considered the others and how they might have affected their first blush of intimacy.

21

the garden

Flames reached out beyond the circle of the pit and licked at their feet. Madeline felt elevated by the fire, felt she was the owl in her barn again but not cowering. She was free in the night, soaring through the darkness, the silent hunter. With the addition of something retrieved from her bag, a dried and tangled concoction of leaves and flowers, Buki turned the pit into an angry ball of amber smoke. Flames kissed at the fringes and then retreated into the murky tempest. Carmen filled her nostrils with the aroma and let its effervescence engulf her. Angel wings or wings of a giant bird spread out from behind and she was exalted.

Buki sat in a meditation and murmured the heavy tones of a mantra and the other women began to move sympathetically. Everything was vapour, the ground disappeared beneath them, the flames tantalised, the air electrified. Madeline removed her clothes. She felt suffocated by them and longed to indulge the velvety lick of the smoke. She began to reach into the mist seeking herself. The incantation brought to life a new Madeline, a shadow, a doppelgänger, a spirit dancer, elusive. She reached into the mirror and gathered up handfuls of smoke and the tricky, vapourous reflection would skip away. She marvelled at the magic.

Madeline could be heard bursting out in fits of giggles. Carmen had become the angel. She hovered above the flames. She tamed the fire with gentle whips of her wings. She gave Madeline sweet and pious looks full of love for what Nature is capable of. She counted stars and blessed the moon. Madeline caught hold of something; it was Carmen. She pulled her in, fascinated that the elusive shadow was now tangible.

The angel took the owl into her keep. Safe and warm within the scented confine. It was a sacred space within a space. Her wings circled about the small-feathered creature. The little owl's great eyes surrendered their innocence to the deep loving blackness of the angel's eternal knowing. They rested.

22

genesis

We entered a space, a room with four doors. I had glimpsed its blue interior the day before. Ahead of me a larger door, metallic and designed to be impenetrable, stood ominously. It was a door designed to keep something out or something in, something that one may or may not need a microscope to see. I contemplated its foreboding presence for a duration, an extended pause, a stretch. It went on, I fidgeted, we looked at each other and then at the space. Our heads full of the same quandary - is this cold, cobalt crypt really what they had in mind to enable the transaction? Should this inhospitable abode be the place where our passion made its pioneering statement? No bed? No comforts? No further instruction? No preamble or ceremony? No Dulaney? I asked the question by moving closer to Miriam. She was hesitant. She was innocent and acted an inexperienced affection; it was vulnerability. It was the first display of weakness I had seen her endure and I was discomforted. The second door opened and Jane entered.

Miriam and I were caught in an embrace. Another protracted pause ensued. Miriam and I separated and monitored Jane as she registered the features of the space. Now there were three in the room and I was inclined to absurdity - had there been some details of this encounter that my reasoning had not connected with? I assumed there would be only one or, at the very least one at a time? Would I be expected to father more than one Frankenstein? Be companion to more than one bride of science? Was this scientific elaboration to be informed by promiscuity? I asked the question by moving closer to Jane and she quizzed me with hard glances. The door burst open again and Michael appeared.

Anna came in by the third door and finally Will entered. Our suspicion then migrated towards the fourth wall and its large metal door. It stood as a mute answer to an unspoken question and yet we floundered. I put my lascivious miscalculations soundly aside. Will provided,

"I expected God's waiting room to be furnished but I can't tell you why."

He had managed to do what he was innately inclined to do and do with humour, what humour may be inclined to do innately, remind us of our very cerebral connection to this enterprise.

I began to feel vulnerable. There would be no safety in numbers here. This evaluator room was in free-fall. Miriam, the bravest, stepped towards the metal plate and reached out. It was indicative of a first encounter. When the alien craft lands and before the doors open, with a touch the question is asked, is it real? She was full of curiosity and her reach was informed by a strange kind of placating welcome. Her fingers made contact and it cracked open. The motorised action made the door appear unstoppable and we all moved back unnecessarily. We searched the space behind and could see only white brilliance and Will's waiting room comment reverberated poignantly.

Anna moved past Miriam and was the first to enter the space. Women are braver and not because they take risks but because they know risk like they know pain. It must be faced and always exists for a reason. We existed for a reason and given our penchant for curiosity there would be nothing else for it but to violate the breach.

It was a breaching and a kind of rebirthing but not necessarily in that order. We were not entering a free space. We were entering a kind of claustrophobic awakening. We were entering a womb where we would be expected to shelve the seeds of humanity and give ourselves entirely to the sustainable management of their dormancy.

We were infants coming into the light for the first time, our eyes full but chary and time stood still. Slowly I made out the open space of a common area surrounding a large white table. Behind was a library and next to that a preparation area with breakfast bar and white goods. The corridor to the left, I would soon discover, led to a series of bedrooms and a large recreation area.

This space, the choreographed manner in which the door closed behind us and the assumed isolation was disconcerting. Our incarceration had been secured effortlessly. We had been cajoled into this prison with promises of an obscure immortality and our science-saturated narcissism had been used as a blindfold.

We had not thought to query the obvious. The long drive across the reservation? The bunker style design of The Facility? The oppressive military presence? Not one of many relative anomalies had caused any of us to challenge the authority that we had subsequently surrendered to. For all we knew this blandly appointed space might be a gas chamber and we might be the first in a never ending line of intellectuals who have been assigned to extinction. We might be the test subjects for a process of extermination that allows a paranoid, power hungry establishment to control the dispersion of quality genetic material.

I didn't panic. I didn't fix my focus onto the air vents anticipating the vapours of a lethal gas to come hissing forth. But I noted our gullibility and, subsequently, an individuals inability to respond to doubt when the dynamics of the group intervene. It cannot be underestimated this group effect. Persuasion needs numbers and ignorance. Ignorance is the binding agent and the common ground upon which many may stand and default to a raw survivalist notion that there is strength in numbers. Hitler knew this too well. He made an entire nation comfortable in their ignorance. More than that, he put smart uniforms on their ignorance and paraded it before them. He had made them own it like patriotism.

We had been allowed to let our hubris inform our ignorance and consequently we had surrendered all liberties. One man in a room is art, two is politics, three is a movement and more? Flocks of sheep. We had become the flock following the call of science and fiction, like Lamarckian Lemmings.

Presently, we charged the strength of our number with the mission to eradicate ignorance. Some went into the deep recesses of the library and others explored the wings. We separated into expeditions without the need for direction and similarly we returned to the common area and proceeded to report our findings. Our common sense of curiosity synchronised our actions and familiarised our purpose. We understood the desires of the scientific mind to understand all that could be understood and question everything that understanding required us to question. Because of these characteristics we were ideal candidates for *The Genesis Program*.

I remained in the common area and was the first to see those words written on the document. The thin file sat next to a copy of The Daily Telegraph. Typed inauspiciously on the file's grey carded cover was the word *Genesis*. The physical weight of the file told me nothing about the magnitude of its contents. But as I raised it into my field of vision I knew that I had discovered a single point of contact that would unravel all the mysteries of this bunker. The solemn remembrance of the closing vault tolled as I read, it acted as a knell marking our decent into hell.

Miriam was the first to report back and gave a detailed account of the library, the absurd enormity of it and the endless number of referenced subjects. Michael gave an account of the accommodation wing and Jane explained that a food preparation area had been provided and was more than adequately appointed. None had noticed that I had become dumb and that the tool that might unlock the mystery of our incarceration was an unassuming document uneasily in my possession.

Will was the first; he noticed the newspaper. He picked it up bemused and then his focus hardened. He said,

"John? Are you able to explain why this paper is dated tomorrow and why the front page suggests that we might all meet a predetermined end complements of a military mishap?"

He threw the paper down to reveal the headline, *KIA: Best and Brightest*. It was now clear to all that I indeed knew the answer to this and many other quandaries. I hesitated - had we been sent to a death chamber? If so, being shown how the media will remember us seemed cruel and unusual punishment and decidedly redundant. Cruel and unusual as it so happened, was an understatement. I held the truth in my clammy hand and it was much worse than any paranoid musing might surmise. So I hesitated, then chose to read from the document directly,

"Welcome to The Genesis Program. You have been selected to occupy this purpose built facility

because you represent the very best in human design. It is in the interest of the free world that a living anthropological and biological ark be established whereby, in the face of an extinction event, the continuation of the species may be assured. You are required to remain in this facility for a period of fifteen years. Upon the conclusion of this term you will be given new identities and returned to civilian life. It is imperative that you make use of the resources provided to advance your knowledge of humankind.

The occurrence of an event will cause the doomsday siren to sound and the facility will adopt quarantine conditions. Exiting the bunker at anytime is impossible; a safe exit will only be achieved at the conclusion of your prescribed term. Automated test stations will indicate if the outside environment is habitable; it may take many years for decontamination to occur.

It will be necessary for calculations to be made determining correct procreation rates relative to the degree of contamination. These calculations and other determinations can be made with the aid of the Genesis manual located at GN 142.7 in the reference library.

The governments of Great Britain and the United States of America acknowledge your sacrifice and hope that you understand the importance of your mission. For security and operational purposes your deaths will be falsely accounted for. Tomorrow's Newspapers will indicate a tragic military accident. Your respective families will be notified in a dignified manner. The expense of all appropriate condolences and funeral arrangements will be the burden of a grateful government."

23

the saviour

Jentz had taken to early morning exercise. He was alone in the mist. He hid within the cloud; he had been hiding for a decade. Here in Oxford, by the water, across the fields, among the trees Nature became an ally and aided his anonymity. He felt Mutter-erde had brought him into a homely place, free of judgment, unfettered by the past. Though it was reminiscent of that night, the night he had crossed the darkness and found sanctuary in a barn and the company of a frightened girl. Nature now worked to remind him of its power to seclude and it was reassuring.

This would be a good place to die, he brooded, with Nature's sympathy and memory, alone but not lonely. He stood by the stream. It was shallow but it didn't stop him from imagining his lifeless body moving with the current. It filled him with freedom so he closed his eyes and believed that he might fall forward and be taken under. The splash was distinctive, his musing was vivid, he opened his eyes. It was real. The bank opposite, a body, naked, lifeless bobbed to the surface.

He couldn't swim but there was no need. The water filled his boots and came up past his knee. He waded his way towards the ghostly figure, a woman. She was pale and unconscious. Hair clung to her face. He took her up under the arms and heaved himself and her on to the bank. He applied some pressure to the thorax. He massaged the vital areas, sought a pulse and made medical enquiries. She was breathing but her lips were blue and she needed warmth. His coat was dry and he wrapped her in it. Her body responded to the warmth and receded into the cocoon. Who was this little snail with her head on his lap?

He began to work her hair into some organisation. It was heavily scented and a wet smoky essence gave him a moment's dizziness. Her eyes were revealed, then her lips, her nose and her neck, Madeline? The forest floor cracked. He saw the figures of women, one tall and lean, the other shorter and more round. They caught sight of him and rushed forward. He had to force himself to take a breath, remind himself of himself. Was it Madeline? The girl in the barn? He thought to say something in French; he thought to seek confirmation. He thought he might incriminate himself. He thought Nature is cruel and that his anonymity had been felled.

The two women arrived and he explained that he had heard a splash and had provided assistance. The ladies fussed and roused. Madeline rose to her feet, opened her eyes and was ushered off. Jentz thought to follow but they gestured otherwise. The taller, dark haired one explained that he might collect his jacket, she told him where and thanked him. Madeline had steadied herself against his arm. She had just now felt his strength and she had whispered *thank you*. He had heard an accent, not discernible but it was Madeline. She had looked at him and his blood went cold.

24

in the beginning

Shock infuses like an anaesthetic but it makes you vividly conscious. Its surgeon, charged with extracting every feeling of security and physical assuredness from you, begins his work and somewhere deep inside you scream for him to stop. He works quickly and disables your responses. You are being turned off from the inside one fuse at a time. No one said anything initially and the silence made it worse. With the passing of every silent second the realness of the mission seemed more palpable. Time continued to pass and the moment when it might have been right for someone to challenge the legitimacy of the document came and went. Next came the moment for anyone to say anything, anything at all that would help alleviate the stupefaction and still nothing.

The seconds raced by and my instincts encouraged a self-analysis. It was a vital sign, an indication that I was still functioning, conscious and aware. It distracted me and stabilised. It occurred to me how true it is that, with the prostituting of luminance perspective will deceive. It is as contrasting as night and day, literally. The moon masks the familiar and the sun gives us an X-Ray view of a vacuum. We had endured a posturing of prisms through which we now saw the fractions of light that made up destiny, defined by incarceration. It was a very scientific befuddlement informed by a very befuddled kind of freedom, one that comes with having all your decisions made for you.

Carmen...? She would be free now. This sudden stop, this unexpected expectation would be her ultimate liberation. This was my first, telling reaction. She may have been the one Medicine determined as incapable, but it was very real to me then that it was I who was interfering with conception. For some time I had suspected that to blame only one of us for our childless state was misguided and naive. It was a combined effect attached to the psychology of our biology. There was nothing disparaging to be said for the way we loved each other. However, I do not believe that sanguine qualities displayed in a couple's interactions need necessarily coincide with what they are capable of achieving biologically. We functioned well as a team but Nature required us to make no lasting contribution and we were politely powerless in the face of it. I understand that I am not exactly referring to a scientific phenomenon. The kind of incompatibility I am referring to links back to a time before time, when destiny was being programmed and God was still scratching his head. Was Genesis giving her the opportunity to discover the compatibility she needed and deserved?

I stopped myself from experiencing the sadness I felt. I would miss Carmen terribly and my heart was breaking. I stopped myself because even though we had an endless supply of time it was clear that at that very moment, we needed to give ourselves the word of action,

"Do we stage a challenge...do we rebel?" I said, affecting some pragmatism.

"It might be expected?" Anna asked rhetorically.

She was sangfroid and critically so and she was right. This entire endeavour maybe a ruse of sorts designed to elicit aggression. This document and this stage might exist to test some base human resolve. In another facility down the road another group may likewise be secured. But they might have been coached, counselled, told what to expect, been given some psychology and a choice. They would be the informed group *A* and we would be the deep-end-first group *B*. Comparisons would be made, psychological observations attested to and ultimately the question could be answered, *is a punch-in-the-realities method a better way to man an ark than a more informed, congenial approach?*

Will heard this question and the others like it hidden within Anna's posturing and offered to breakdown the first analysis,

"We are alone and nothing exists beyond the boundary of this commune. This is what we are asked to accept. We are expected to believe that humanity's degradation is, as of this moment, possessed by cataclysmic malevolence. We must accept that the controllers of this facility and the powers that put us here are subject to an enduring winter. They are stepping out into a new world, much like we are, and they are hoping that the The Genesis Program will save mankind. Consider for a moment the resources, the time and the innovation that has been employed to secure our inclusion. We may have been tricked into this space, our ambition exploited in the process but, essentially, we have no one to blame but ourselves. The cold, rude way in which we have been imprisoned is extreme but it will bolster the fortitude we'll require to rebuild civilisation."

He took possession of the document, gazed at it fatefully and to himself, but for the benefit of all, he concluded,

"We must resolve gloriously to survive and to do so effectively we must correct, in a gloriously human and contrite manner, the arrogance that put us here."

In one concise portrayal Will had managed to exemplify a quality that surely informed his selection. It was a beautiful marriage of ideology and pragmatism. There was nothing more to be said at that time because we very pragmatically and ideologically agreed with him. This facility was unique, its inhabitants were unique and its cocooning motives were very unique and a rational reaction to a world gone mad.

Unlike our freedom irony had not been left at the door. Will was right, hubris had invited us into the space and we gladly accepted the offer. But our

122

egos had been sent to the dunce's corner and to suppose that we should imitate God was beyond comprehension. Simultaneously however, we had been prompted to act as creator, as the champions of a new civilisation, as the founding entities of a braver new world, as born-again Gods? We had to be contrite but also accept that we had been forced into a new hubris, a very pragmatic version.

25

prodigal

Jentz could suffer the loss of his jacket; the store in town had another just like it. He had endured a trauma; her resurrection meant his condemnation. He divined the details of the dream; his boots had charred as they dried on the hearth. He discovered the house was consistent with the directions given; he made furtive appearances. He was sure the authorities would seek him out soon; Madeline would attest. The war had not been forgotten, his lie would be exposed and he thought he should run. But the hope that he might be liberated from the guilt held him regardless of the consequences; such was the nature of his torment. Madeline might provide him with a means to manage the madness beyond morphine, a final and absolute penance. He risked exposure. One afternoon he spied them, the taller woman who had given him the directions and Madeline, she clung to the lady's arm. She was full of childish joy and he envied her freedom.

• • •

Madeline was in no doubt as to the identity of

her saviour; she guarded the secret. It filled her with power and she had Nature to thank for delivering him; she would bide her time. She had seen the weariness in his face and knew time had weakened his resolve. She knew that face very well. She had kept the memory of it alive. She had reached out and felt its contours. In dreams she had seen it twist with the sting of death and rest. She had taken his final peace gently into her lap, as he had done for her. She had kissed him and surrendered him to the angels. In dreams she had played out her revenge, it was no longer a dream. She admired his jacket hanging in Carmen's hall wardrobe; her caress was inquisitive and provided all her senses with affirmation. It was a glass slipper, a singing siren bringing him to her.

●　　●　　●

It was dusk as Jentz approached the door. He was numb. The door felt impenetrable as he sounded his arrival. Footsteps could be heard, it opened and the dark haired women appeared,

"Hello, can I help you?"
He faltered, inexplicably fearful of the fraudulence his native tones might portray; he remembered the defector he once was and worried - will I ever give up the shame,

"Hello," he responded, "I am Jentz...I believe you have my jacket?"

"But of course, please come in, I am Carmen."
Her warmth was palpable; she was ingratiating,

"How do I thank you? I was hopping to have the opportunity before now."

She retrieved his forsaken jacket and placed it

on a hook by the door,

"Please go through to the kitchen," she volunteered.

He proceeded further into the house. The kitchen was an open space and he didn't notice her initially. Madeline stood near the sink with a cup of tea. The reunion placed them into a stasis that may have endured an eternity if it were not for Carmen,

"Please let me pour you a tea. I believe you have already met Madeline? I do not know the words to express the intensity of my gratitude. If you had not...then I..." She took a moment to exhale the emotion.

"Yes, I am most grateful," Madeline could not look him in the eye but the sentiment was sincere.

He was led into a sitting room where another silence endured.

"...Jentz? It is German?" Carmen asked knowingly.

"...Yes," his apprehension checked her.

Carmen persisted however, and began soliciting some chat learning that Jentz was a doctor working at the University. Madeline listened.

She knew his voice, the gentle modulation, the same bewitching tones that had made her an ally in his abandonment. She felt his shyness and recalled the contradiction. She remembered how the knife had twisted. She recognised the sadness recessed in his eyes, a war weary gaze that told of too much death, it encouraged images of the boy he was. She remembered her vow to seek revenge and she recalled the night in the forest and her not so ill fated splash into the river; Nature had delivered him.

"Oh! How very wrong of me," Carmen rose, "I have promised you tea and that is all. How wrong! A promise tastes nothing like the tea itself," she skipped across the room.

Jentz stood. He did not wish to delay his departure. He made a motion towards the door and thought to say something.

"Jentz you must stay. Carmen, I shall make the tea."

With the authoritative treatment of these utterances Madeline made all polite hesitation evaporate. In one decisive motion she attained control and compliance. She marched sternly towards Jentz. She gestured that she might take his coat. Carmen had failed to collect it earlier. Her customs had been corrupted by confusion. He was a visitor unusually in possession of more than one outer garment. He gave it up sheepishly, like a husband might give up his wet socks to a disgruntled wife perplexed that he should bring his mess indoors.

Jentz had felt the full force of Madeline's insistence and also had sensed something ominous hidden within it. He sat and considered his confusion. Carmen had been similarly curtailed and likewise was aware of a baleful undertone.

Madeline hung the coat by the door next to the other he had given up to save her. She reflected - in this coat he has come as the condemned and in the other he came as saviour, but which shall be his shroud?

From the kitchen she went directly to the back

door. The sitting room light illuminated the garden path and Carmen's silhouette was set within its frame. Madeline followed a line of shadow as Jentz had taught her ten years previous, the irony was acknowledged incidentally. The garden shed was dark and she used her hands as eyes to seek out the small apothecary case. She knew the vial. She removed the lid and recognised the sweet deception of the deadly plant. She clasped the bottle and closed the door silently.

Carmen continued to entertain the reticent Jentz. He was forced to confess that he knew of her husband. It was a piece of common ground upon which they could loiter indifferently. From the corner of her eye she noticed Madeline in the garden, motionless, mute, hypnotised possibly, exposed precisely and a vial in her hand. Carmen suppressed a suddenly stab of unease.

● ● ●

Madeline had been waiting for this moment for a lifetime it seemed. She made her way up the path from the shed. She had seen his sheepish looks, his reassuring ways. She had heard the stories full of the love he had for his sister. She had loved her family and he had loved deeply. She had watched him move through the battle lines, cheating them both out of death, and she had felt his hand take her into his safety. She knew what it was to feel that strange manipulation. She knew he had worked magic on her, that they had both been young and innocent. She had bid him farewell and felt a yearning. That was ten years ago. She had let her anger keep his memory alive and she was grateful for that fateful hate. She had held onto the image. She had kissed those lips a thousand times and wished him peace. She had...loved?

Preoccupation had stolen her senses and left her exposed in the yard. Had Carmen seen her? Recollections of the lantern, the gunfire, the deadly consequence of her distraction ten years previous, provoked repentance to which she responded directly. She made for the kitchen. The water was hot, the cups and saucers readily at hand, the instruments of death were all conveniently arranged. She inclined - to go into the sitting room empty handed is to be empty hearted and that would be grossly misleading. She made the brew. It was ritualistic. She had mixed the poison many times in numerous fantasies. She had seen him take it to his lips.

The cup trembled in the saucer. Carmen rose. She hoped to arrest Madeline, meet her at the door and interrupt the exchange. Jentz felt that if he could take the tea quickly he might be on his way ending his immense discomfort. Madeline didn't so much give him the tea it was more that he took it from her. Before any hesitation could be endured he had taken the saucer, the cup and a healthy gulp. Carmen gasped, stepped forward and slapped the remnants of the concoction from his hand. Jentz recoiled. The air was infused with the rich aroma of the tea and instantly Carmen recognised...Camomile and honey?

Confusion pervaded. Madeline felt it well inside her like a storm-surge. Everything seemed to quiver and shake. She couldn't run, the time was now, ten years was long enough. She gave Carmen a look full of gratitude and love. Carmen reciprocated incomprehensibly. Jentz floundered and then met Madeline's teary gaze. She stepped forward and with a tentative advance touched his face. It was alive and warm and she longed to take it, nurture it, cherish it. He had seen her as a girl. He had seen her be shunted into adulthood and he had said a prayer at the heads of her beloved parents. He had risked his life to give her freedom and he knew her better than he could possibly understand. He took her into his embrace and allowed her to feel him, to feel love. He wanted her to feel everything at that moment, that he was real and with her and understood and would love her and never stop.

● ● ●

Carmen knew that sometimes fate fêted felicity but that this Jentz should be the anonymous defector Madeleine had admonished in dreams, who had been her saviour ten years previous, seemed ludicrous. Then she recalled the writer she might know as the father of her children and his timely departure and mused - with fact time will patinando and fate will parry it with fiction. The winner will be the more obscure and their prize? Potential.

26

kingdom come

Evidently eternity is finite. It lasts for exactly seven days. We heard the mechanism release, felt the pressure bleed and a déjà vu. Those of us in the common room at the time turned to the solid steel structure that had sealed in our eternity a week earlier and with a clunk the door opened...!

•   •   •

I struggled initially, to understand what we had demonstrated with the endurance of seven of the longest days of our lives. Clearly the question had been asked, *could humans be tucked away like catalogued specimens and be relied upon to present society's blueprints to a blank canvas future, and not loose their minds as they waited?* I struggled because even with the end of these seven days I could, in no way, inspire a response to that question. I was in short supply of objectivity but I was confident that we had given an account of next to nothing.

Sophistication is a kind of nothingness. Was this the motivation? Was this entire enterprise an exercise in doing something purely because absolute power may generate absolute belief in nothing, in the existence of a perfectly impossible vacuum? It had been demonstrated by war that absolute power buys absolutism. The idea that subjectivity might be enabled towards the flouting of liberties must have made the powerful dizzy with malevolent anticipation. For the briefest of global moments it became a mark of superiority that a Government may exploit its own constituents towards sophistic ends. Behavioural Science was a new battlefield upon which world forces would attempt to argue that mine was bigger than yours. Or ours is a more disturbed kind of manipulation than yours could ever hope to be.

Whatever the motivation The Genesis Program seemed to me like an excessively elaborate means to ego driven vagueness. It was caveman science motivated by the premise that by adding one thing to another a reaction might precipitate. There's no prediction, no hypothesis to test, it's simply stand-behind-the-protective-screen-wait-and-watch science. Many virtues were lost in the stupefying story arch that was the Second World War; some were never recovered. But I had hoped science would resurrect its ethics. But no, instead it found opportunity and it felt fear, adventurous bedfellows and explosive cellmates.

● ● ●

The door opened like a lung and respired. Miriam, the first to arrive was the first again. With little ceremony she approached the door. I imagined that she might assign the entire experience to a very

132

analytical part of her brain. She hadn't once made a display of it but our rude incarceration and our precipitous liberation must have caused her some annoyance. But vexation for her was nothing more than a spark in a neural process that would ultimately lead to the creation of a hypothesis and copious amounts of devoted sophistication.

But there was another side. These seven days had forced connections to be formed like a child associating or a bird learning its song. If nothing else we had demonstrated the propensity for humans to form bio-organisations or *organism-isations*. Miriam, whether she liked it or not, would now have a part of her memory allocated to the organism The Genesis Program forced us to become. It is this lingering reminder that may surface from time to time, for apparently no reason, which will shudder through us a sensation that confuses and subdues. Genesis took us to the edge and beyond, into a sacred space where science and humanity attempt to converge. It is not an impossible amalgam but it is impossible to maintain without sustaining an injury. It is a very human kind of affliction that saddens the heart a little and deadens the senses somewhat. We were shell-shocked by a cold and invisible war, frightened by what might have been and by what might not have been.

Miriam had masterfully controlled the degree to which she was detached demonstrating an astute self-awareness. But now she approached the threshold and hesitated, it was unbecoming. She turned; there was something uncharacteristic about it, uninhibited. She was responding to a different kind of honesty. It did not require theorems, substantiations or empirical rigidity and it was not detached. It was an unqualified response. It was a smile. It was the first I had seen and it might have been a thousand words. It might have been our only truth. It lives vividly in my memory and remains unreconciled.

27

exodus

Dulaney stood on the far side of the cramped blue room, the same space that had embarrassingly accommodated, seven days previously, a stretching of my salaciousness. He stood at the threshold of the rabbit hole and wanted to know surely, how far did we descend? He stood there as if to ask, *do you wish to blame someone*? And also to answer, *because here I am*. I was the last to leave. I fixed a stare onto his one eye and desired that he had one more upon which I could also focus so he may know the full intensity of my anger. My fist twisted at the end of my arm, my jaw clenched as the image I had evolved of a grieving Carmen dissolved into blind frustration. The words in my head fought to arrange themselves into punches and my legs anticipated the first jut of aggression.

He stood there all in black, hands in pockets, leaning against the far door in a very American manner. He absorbed my scrutiny and then allowed his head to fall back; he was exposed and weary. He looked with his one eye down his nose at me. It was impartial but cautious. It was a look that invited serenity, a very academic kind of calm. There is a peace that exists between scientists, such as we are, that is informed by forbearance. We wait and adjust then assess and then wait some more. The waiting forces the tools of investigation to turn inwards. So he stood there waiting for logic to subdue me, it was a small minute. My jaw relaxed, my fist softened and my mind raced over the details of my week's performance. I was a rat in a cage observed by rats in a maze responding to the fear generated by other rats that were fearful of rats and on it goes. It was a farce and so I laughed. He was not surprised to hear my ejaculations. I cackled, bellowed, cried, rejoiced, collapsed, sighed, screamed and screeched with laughter. It went on endlessly, awkwardly, unprecedentedly and he responded with mute placidity.

I can give no insight into my reaction, beyond acknowledging that we had done much in the pursuit of nothing. Also I had not been entirely convinced. Something about this ark seemed impermanent. The library gave me my first sting of suspicion. To represent all of humanity is a challenging undertaking but this catalogue was implausibly complete. There were archeological holes, historical gaps, biological omissions, political simplifications and an artistic abridgement. Was the future to be informed by an understanding of the world as white, English-speaking people saw it? Carmen would have made better use of the cavernous space and replaced a black and white photograph of an Inca icon with a faithful imitation. It was not a sincere representation of the entire human story; it was a cross section.

My suspicion was also aroused because I didn't belong, none of us did. I didn't want to be dead to my family, to my Carmen, even to our nonexistent, bureaucratically besieged dog or to our unborn children. When that door closed I expected to consider all manner of rebellion, which I did. But beyond that, innately, after the fear and anger had been accounted for, I simply could not accept that I would be trapped in that test tube for eternity. There was something about the way the cups sat uneasily on the saucers, the way the plastic chairs flexed with our weight and how the can-opener occasionally lost its bite. Everything appeared staged. The water from the tap gushed like a spring stream; it aroused a rhetorical reservation - how would the resources of a compromised future be best managed? I am wise with hindsight and without it I was uneasy. But the collage of incongruence formed during those seven days still hangs vividly on the wall of my intuition.

28

the children

We stood in an arrangement dictated to us by the camera. Our children, too young to know that a photograph requires some sense of occasion, stared up at us blankly. The formless countenance babies adopt with apparent callousness attempts to make a mockery of politeness and I am momentarily aware how ridiculous these staged moments are. Youth has wisdom because of ignorance and a baby's ignorance is as expansive as the universe and subsequently, encompasses all. I considered that God might be a baby. But he is not a baby, a baby is the effect, life is the cause and God is time allowing for the cause to have an effect.

Carmen halted proceedings by leaping out of the frame but not before the shutter was struck. The photographer wound the film and disguised his frustration with rehearsed politeness.

"Rama, Rama come here boy. We must have Rama," she called him over and he obliged with the submissive enthusiasm indicative of Greyhounds.

We arranged ourselves again, the dog, Carmen

and I with a child each, Madeline, with her child and Jentz. Before we were given to another distraction the shutter clicked, the film wound and the posturing for posterity's sake ended.

I looked at Carmen and saw the woman I fell in love with who had become the mother she wanted to be and I was grateful they were the same person. I had searched and so had she and in each other we found the beginning and the end of something. We were very much on the same side of a beautiful disappointment.

● ● ●

Everyday I feel the nagging melancholy of disappointment. Disappointed in myself for not being a better husband, for not responding promptly to a letter, for not writing more, for not being able to conjure more inspiration, for allowing my ideas to be only what they need to be and not always what they want to be. In the face of my perceived success disappointment constantly needs management. Everyday brings new disappointments forcing me to ask - why can't I have the world? Find more time to be at home? Type faster? Draw upon an unlimited supply of ingenuity?

I cannot have the world and so disappointment must be managed and it must be managed in an affirming manner otherwise there is no meaning. We are here essentially, to be challenged and if fortune favours us it shall be a fulfilling experience. We exist as proof to an affected universe that life is a constant energy as time determines and, so long as time is determined, energy will be motivated to formulate. God planted a seed and gave the energy of the heavens, of the expansion and retraction a form. One that would move with the changes of time and we call it life.

We cannot be given the world because we are the gift. And we receive small incentives encouraging us to embody the gift that *process* receives from *time*. We are the sacrifice and for that we receive communion. We are given togetherness and through the sharing of experience we can gain access to worlds within worlds and time can be dissolved.

• • •

As I stood there with my family and friends a long awaited clarity moved me. It is a source of great pride to me that I have learnt that managing disappointment puts me in contact with others. That I choose to foster a sense of community and share my life with other human beings, allows me to manipulate a response to life's disparagements. It fills me completely with satisfaction that I should choose to placate apprehension and disperse dissonance by enjoying the loving embrace of unity. The children, the man and his wife may never have come into a happy happenstance if it were not for disappointment, if it were not for the gloriousness of God's challenge and the impertinence of time.

• • •

When I think of it now, The Institute, The Facility, The Genesis Program and my ark companions, it is her smile that I see. Miriam's

140

beguiling grin, a Mona Lisa snub, as she exited Genesis. It was a smile that I might have fallen in love with. It might have forced me to speculate endlessly, gloriously and it was, and always will be, the end as I know it. End.

Days of Ark

• Day 2 •

How were we expected to endure this dry winter? With the condensation of purpose to sustain us? With the purification of incarceration to reprogram us? With the repetition of meaning to entrance us? Yes.

The day after brought with it reflections, as if from a still ocean, giving us a penetrating sense of what we were. Sleep had been replaced by cataleptic denial. I woke thinking Carmen might be lying next to me. One day into eternity and I was compelled to consider the person I *was*. I had left him only yesterday, behind that steel trap and he was already distant. Everyday hence would soon be a yesterday imbrued with unfulfilled potential and yet everyday brought us one step closer to fulfilling a glorious potential.

Michael rose on the second day and made vigorous use of the exercise room. Others watched in wonderment. His physique was envious and I delighted at how he might combat the ageing of his abilities, I would have the time to regard it. I concluded that he would weather it well. However, I was caused to recall Narcissus and his fated obsession with image. Michael gave us the gift of clarity as he persisted with agendas, routines and the preservation of life.

142

• Day 3 •

We needed vantages, somewhere from where we could take in the true scope of our commitment. We needed to know what our sacrifice meant. We were underground and we were *underground*. It was a compounding arrangement that blinkered our odyssey. The ship of our humanity would be flown into the unknown by the unknowing through the immovable.

Portals of hope opened by philosophy were our only consolation. Discussions surrounding certain subjects were smothered sophistically. These bemusements found a limited audience; others went to the library or their rooms for silence. Other topics suffused, were given space and pause and frames of reference. These became meditations that reverberated with the heavy presence of the ground in which we were entombed. From the earth came life. We were the new founders and from the earth we would come bearing life but when, how, in what form, from whom and to where? Questions without answers that put us into benign contemplations.

Will would shift perspective, regularly interrupting our festered silences. He regarded the landscape of our cerebral what-notting with the considered eye of a scientist. He would posture that evolution was *The Entity* and longed for our continued involvement. He would suggest that the force that led us into Genesis was self-devised. He would lead us through a cogitation, reveal the unexpected and then take us beyond. His knowledge of the natural world kept us from dismissing the sophistic and caused us to stretch our make-up. Michael had given us the means to physical sustenance and Will sustained our minds with youth.

• Day 4 •

The days were organised carefully into light and dark and the circles of sentiment were trapped in similar movements. However, there was a disconnect. I don't like Mondays and everyday was Monday. What happens when everyday is like the next and the next day is like the rest to come and time is replaced with an impossible purpose? Stasis.

The fourth day brought with it a sense of true repetition. The formula for the future was becoming fixed and consisted of impulse driven ebbs.

Jane knew we were creating small circles of concentration inclined to become increasingly smaller. The pattern needed extrusion and her response was enigmatic.

"Let us be the surf," she said. "Let us be the wave upon the tide. Lets us be the tide that watches the stars and carries eddies, eddies like the wheels in a clock. We are at the will of seven, let the number seven inform the helix of our perpetuity."

With this piece of confusion she had entranced us. She went on to explain,

"Seven days will become seven of seven and this will be our pattern. There is nothing beyond this except that we should measure its effect. The days will be twenty-three hours long, this is more consistent."

She filled our minds with a quandary. It was a

disturbance that lifted our thoughts out of their centric habits. She understood that order needs chaos. She taught us that monotony need not be predictable and order need not be formulaic.

• Day 5 •

Silence, familiar but uneasy. I sensed an atmosphere of caution. The silence penetrated the walls of the bunker. It came from within the earth. My regard of this day's hesitation needed careful consideration but first I considered my companions.

Our noises were unintelligible. We were reluctant to share the percussions of routine. It was more than privacy it was clandestine. I risked exposure. I stepped out into the hallway; it was a void. In the common area a shuffling could be detected, a decoy of normalcy could be felt, a lure to trap me. I proceeded carefully. I knew the cunning of the crowd. I had seen the glances going back and forth as the measures of man were made. We would have a confrontation. The predators would be determined, the defenceless exposed and the flighty fingered. But I would be the shadow.

My pallid presence could easily be disregarded, my feline felicity would bewitch. I would creep past their business. She was foraging, Anna the forager, fragile but fecund. This Nature's child will meet the shadowed prowler. I circled as she fossicked for nourishment, for something to break the fast.

"What means you, spectre?" She said without raising her eyes.

What stealth was this? I had been detected and her intelligence was beyond my intelligence to detect.

"I am seeking arousal," I responded sheepishly.

I crept out from the shadow. She sat a bowl of something down, took a mouthful and regarded me with sleepy aplomb.

"I bet you are," she said between slurps and then a moment's distraction encouraged,

"I can't tell the time, the time as it really is. I can't look out and see it. We can't see time, no windows, no sun, no moon. All I have is this skin on the back of my hands, this soft bit here where the cracks are forming."

She returned to her breakfast and I returned to the shadow.

• Day 6 •

The new beginning will require a fresh injection of data. She would give herself to the purpose with a clinical mode of execution. This was my hypothesis; it was innocuous. To test the proposition however, would bring to light an absolute truth. Men and women differ; I felt obligated to make certain determinations. I am inclined, by instinct, to regard women, to consider the proportions and assess the possibilities. I did however, only have eyes for Carmen, I felt this distinctively. It was a conscious decision to begin to see Miriam for more than first impressions demanded.

There certainly was no mistaking the rude

attraction I felt, but she was not personable. My rudimentary reaction had since been tempered by experience and I was caused to consider the Garden of Eden. Was the Garden a symbol of love, the love of loving? Did the Serpent represent the tricky business of cohabitation? Did the Tree of Knowledge represent the branches of communication that need nurturing? Was The Garden story an interpretation of domestic life that begins with the honeymoon and ends with familiarity? Is this what they mean when they say God is love?

Ballroom dancing would be my means. Every experiment needs a catalyst and the Rumba seemed as good a place to start as any. Not that I was fond of dancing but I was guilty by association. Carmen had once enjoyed ambitions that sometimes required my embarrassed collusion. However, I had proven to be less than awkward. I had learnt that dance was a revelation that told you that of yourself which you may yet know not of and that of others, which they know not of themselves. It was time to force everyone to step outside the square, rhythmically.

It began with a haunting timbre echoing from the activity room. I stood expectantly in the middle of the large space. The others were led by their curiosity accordingly. Miriam came in last. I crossed the floor and took her hand. She responded to my confident grasp and we commenced. The others watched with the singularity of scientists. Then hips began to move, feet began to tap. Step, step, pause, slide, turn and sweep. It was fundamental but synchronised. The others fumbled their way through with dedication. The dance of love requires concentration and focus. The steely persistence of a scientist, it appeared to me, had something to teach the most accomplished Ballroomer.

Miriam turned and wiggled, her toe pointed, her lunges were deep and confident. She followed and flowed. The vinyl skipped and silence. We had danced and there appeared to be an amalgam, it had lived within us but it lacked momentum. My experiment informed me that she was inexperienced. She may have found me attractive. She may have sensed synchronicity. She may have entertained possibilities but she was not versed in the language of action and it made me weary to contemplate her education. I was not the first love she needed.

• Day 7 •

On the seventh day a strange kind of acceptance comforted me. I thought about the cycle of things and cycles within cycles - seven days? What does it allow for? What length of time is needed for the mind to turn and come to a new way of looking at the inevitable?

I no longer regarded the solid steel plug that so unceremoniously had cut our umbilical. We were now a mission with objectives and perspective. I felt I was not alone in my new, more levelled view of things. I felt for the first time that the group had been chosen wisely. We could look at each other and begin to do more than reciprocate uneasiness. We were self-assured, hidden in the recesses of expressions were sympathy, respect, truth, wisdom and love.

The daily routine was not yet routine due to a still overwhelming alienation. Order was evolution's reassurance that we might manage the boredom to come. And order was the child our commune had begun to nurture. In different ways we informed obedience and we could begin to see what life might become.

The habits of imprisonment had become the rituals of faith and on day seven I was given to a virtuous interpretation. Purpose, even if that purpose is to wait, becomes an occupation, a sequestering of time, a sacramental penchant, a reason. Purpose is the gift and time is the mantle upon which it sits, collecting the dust of integrity. Dust it, give it a polish, take a little pride, pause for admiration and let the integrity accumulate once more. Our purpose was not infected by resignation; hope lingered. It was not befuddled by regret. It was a default; a state of human being-ness where being human was the only alternative. With the coming of this seventh day we were become predictable and it was glorious.

Acknowledgements

There are some people who deserve special thanks for their contribution, influence, suggestions and clairvoyance. Rose Chambers, thank you for your devoted edit and for permitting one or two more semicolons than I know you would normally be inclined. Moira Higgins, thank you for your annotations and informed enthusiasm. Lorraine and Bob McDonald, thank you for your early intervention and astute appraisal. You helped make it everything it needed to be and all that I wasn't aware it could be. Jaymie Ling, thank you for seeding inspiration and for sharing obscurities, for revealing the world within the world from where this story erupts. Josh Anderson, thank you for having the patience to listen to every word as I read it aloud, ad nauseam. You were not physically in the room at the time; you were on the other side of the country. But in my mind you were with me informing the tone, correcting the truth and plying the humour. Rory Harris, that this acknowledgement is so embalmed with fate is surely consistent with your erudition and spirit. Your first utterance to me informed this work, I recall it distinctively and I continue to listen. Your influence on this text is both specific and suffuse for which I am immensely grateful. Simone, my love, my worth, thank you. Without you I am whimsy, I am humourless, I am wretched and I am halved. To my mother Margie, thank you for your inspiration and truth. If I were to embody bravery and talent with half as much verve as you are disposed I would consider myself immensely privileged. I have often only had words to give in return for much generosity, thank you for receiving them.

www.ingramcontent.com/pod-product-compliance
Lightning Source LLC
Chambersburg PA
CBHW032205190626
46810CB00018B/1566